EVOLUTION
SAM KADENCE

Harmony Ink

Published by
Harmony Ink Press
5032 Capital Circle SW
Ste 2, PMB# 279
Tallahassee, FL 32305-7886
USA
publisher@harmonyinkpress.com
http://harmonyinkpress.com

Evolution
Copyright © 2013 by Sam Kadence

Cover Art by Paul Richmond
http://www.paulrichmondstudio.com

ISBN: 978-1-62380-410-7
Library ISBN: 978-1-62380-924-9
Digital ISBN: 978-1-62380-411-4

Printed in the United States of America
First Edition
May 2013

Library Edition
August 2013

EVOLUTION

CHAPTER 1

Genesis

I GOT into my Honda, revved the engine, and took a sip of the coffee Joel, my bandmate, had given me. It was about as bad as coffee could get. Brown water. Hopefully the crud had some caffeine in it. The concert I had played sucked the energy right out of me, and I desperately needed the get-up-and-go.

I tore into a bag of M&M's with one hand, dropped the contents onto the opposite seat, and began to pop them into my mouth, one by one, as I headed home. The clock on the dashboard read nearly 3:00 a.m., so it was just after ten. Someday I'd get the wiring fixed so I could reset the clock. Hell, maybe someday I'd have enough money to buy a car that set its own damn clock.

At least the streets were clear. Late nights in New York City weren't as wild as the TV made them seem. Or maybe it was just that I lived in the crappy part of town. My own building could have been on the list for most likely to be condemned. Homeless filled the area with their little carts of trash and cardboard houses. Barely a step above them myself, I couldn't pass judgment. Most guys my age still lived at home, so I couldn't complain much. It felt right to move out, especially when I dropped out of high school. Passing the GED made me feel like I wasn't a total loser, but since I wasn't planning on going to college, I couldn't justify mooching off my mom any longer.

The dark, empty streets had a lulling effect. I had to get home before sleepiness took over and the real spooks came out to play. I pressed the gas a little harder, wondering vaguely about the article in today's paper. Some people from an organization called Preservation Group had set some vampires on fire, the seventh attack this month. The teachers in school had never talked much about the group, but the people setting the fire had been kids in their midteens. Guys like me. Well, I guess, not like me.

I wasn't dead or undead, but the hate group didn't seem to have many boundaries it wouldn't cross. Straight, Christian, white folk maybe, but I was none of the above, being Asian American, Buddhist, and gay. If that didn't put me on their radar, the whole "seeing dead people" thing would. Never mind the fact that when I slept I dreamt of graveyards and a girl who seemed to linger between life and death.

Sighing into the night, I hoped for a peaceful trip home to my cat, Mikka.

Somewhere between the entrance to the highway and the back streets to home, a flash of someone in a white shirt bolting in front of the car made me slam the brake to the floor. I jerked the steering wheel to the left, but overcorrected, nearly sending the car into a spin. M&M's hit the dash with loud pings, tires screeched, and scalding brown water poured into my lap. I lost the brake and accidentally hit the accelerator while trying to counter steer out of the spin.

The headlights beamed on a man's astonished face just seconds before I hit him. He rolled up onto the hood. My foot found the brake again, throwing me forward in the seat. The man slid off, lay stunned for a moment, and then sat up slowly. The lights glared into his face, his eyes hidden in the dark. Blood dripped from his scalp.

My whole world stood frozen for that moment. I could barely breathe. My body was stuck in limbo, eyes blinking, heart racing, mind paralyzed in fear.

Finally, the panic gave way to adrenaline. I slammed the gear into park, leapt out, and rounded the car to look at my victim. Crap, my victim. I hit someone with my car. If my heart could beat any harder, I was sure blood would come rushing out of my ears.

"I'm so sorry," I told the guy. He couldn't have been much older than me. "I'll call 911."

From this angle it didn't appear to be all that bad. The blood trickling down his face already began to slow, and he just seemed dazed. His body didn't look all twisted and broken like you'd think someone who got hit by a car would be. He was, however, wearing a dark coat and a long black duster. Not a white tee.

I glared back at the main road where I'd seen someone run in front of me before the accident. If that had been a ghost, then I'd just wrecked my car and almost killed someone for no reason. Sometimes I wished spirits just had flashing signs over their heads saying "already dead."

"What the hell is your problem, kid?" The injured man struggled to get to his feet. The blood at his temple flowed a little faster with the added movement. The glass of the windshield hadn't shattered, for which I was grateful, but he still looked a little worse for wear.

"You shouldn't move." I tried to get him to sit back down. He looked pretty unsteady and gripped my arm to keep upright. "You should sit before you fall over. Let me call for help."

"You weren't going fast enough to squash a bug. What kind of idiot drives on the sidewalk? Were you trying to kill someone? Would you like to get in your car and back over me a few times?"

At least he was talking. That meant no punctured lungs, right? What did those doctor TV shows always say was bad, head trauma? He had that. He stumbled, but I caught him. "Did you see anyone else on the street?" I had to ask. "Like someone in a white shirt?"

"Just you. And I'm pretty sure yours is pink." He grabbed a pack of cigarettes out of his pocket and lit one. The smoke pooled in annoying rings around my head. He relaxed against me, forcing me to take the brunt of his weight. Since I was always the small guy in the room, that was harder said than done.

"It's orange." I flipped out my cell phone to dial the cops. "Just relax, mister. I'll call for help." The dial tone barely buzzed before he had his hand over the receiver, taking the phone away. *What the hell?* "Let me call for help. You could be seriously hurt."

"Only my pride." The heavy glare of headlights made his eyes dark with shadows. "I'm the one who got hit by a car, but you pissed your pants. Is that why you were on the sidewalk? Trying to make it to the bathroom in time? They make a pill for that."

"It's coffee! I thought I saw a man in the road, swerved to miss him, and the coffee spilled!"

He tilted my face up toward his. I could smell the smoke on his breath and the blood from his brow. "You don't smell like alcohol. And your pupils are normal, so no drugs. You could do with a little less glitter and eyeliner. See invisible things often?"

I pulled away, letting him lean against the car, irritated by the tone of his voice. Even now, when the supernatural had become the norm, people still insisted on hiding their heads in the sand. Most of the world was made up of that kind of person. Not my problem, at least most of the time. This guy was probably one of those.

"Get in the car. I'll take you to the hospital." I got in the driver's side, waiting for him to move. The car still ran, even though it had body-sized dent in the hood.

The guy stared in my direction before nodding slightly and getting into the passenger seat. As soon as he closed the door, I was racing toward the hospital at top speed. He gripped his seat belt. Red highlights in his hair reflected color each time we passed a streetlight. I must have glanced his way two dozen times.

"Stop! Just stop the car! You're going to kill us both."

I stomped on the brake. Inertia threw me forward in the seat and made my passenger growl. I let the car crawl its way over to the curb until I could park it out of the way of other vehicles. Only when I cut the engine and took my hands off the wheel did he let go of his seat belt and swept his fingers swept through his hair, long fingers, like those of an artist. I wondered briefly if he'd get mad if I turned on the inside light so I could look at him. But he was glaring at me. The heat of his gaze made my shoulders tense even in the darkness of the car.

"What?" I finally asked.

"You have pink hair."

"So?"

"You're a guy, right? Or an ugly girl with no boobs."

"Guys can't have pink hair?"

"Not can't. Shouldn't."

The dig stung, especially since I'd attempted to dye it red that morning, but the pink was what I'd ended up with. "I change it all the time. Last week it was yellow. I'm a musician, a singer. It's a music thing."

"It looks stupid."

I should have been angrier. Sadly, I sort of agreed, but I didn't have the cash to buy another box of dye to change it until next week. "That's a crappy thing to say to someone who's trying to help you."

"You hit me with your car. A shitty car, at that. Did you buy it at the junkyard? I'm surprised it runs." He flicked the butt of his cigarette out the window and ran his fingers through his hair again. "You never answered my question."

"What question? My car came from a neighbor, not the junkyard." Though, in truth, it was junkyard material.

An attempt to light another cancer stick failed when his lighter wouldn't work. He searched the dash for the car's lighter, but I had thrown it away years ago. "I so need a smoke."

"You should let me take you to the hospital."

"I'm not due for a lobotomy yet." He sat in silence for a bit, staring out the window, then said, "I asked if you often saw stuff that isn't there."

7

The sigh escaped me before I realized we were back to that topic. "No. Everything I see is there. Just because you can't see it, doesn't mean it's not there."

The silence came back and lasted probably five minutes, feeling more like an hour before he moved, getting out of the car. "Get out."

"Why?" I gripped the steering wheel. Being left out in the middle of nowhere without a way home was a very possible option, and one I didn't want. Not even in payback for hitting a man with my car. Getting set on fire or beaten to death 'cause I was different suited me even less. He didn't look like the Preservation Group type, but did anyone really? Guys like me knew when to stay inside, and after dark was one of those times. I'd been shoved in enough lockers and toilets to know better. And those things were mild compared to what I read about in the papers every day.

"'Cause I don't want to die tonight. Give me the keys." He came around the car and stood at my door as I opened it. I left the keys in the ignition. The man motioned to the passenger side. "Get in or I'm leaving without you, kid." He folded his tall frame into the driver's seat and adjusted the seat's position.

"Genesis," I said as I slid into the car on the passenger side. "My name is Genesis. My friends call me Gene." The man stared at me again. I wished I could see him better. "What?"

"I don't care what your name is." He leaned over, yanked the seat belt across my shoulder and over my chest, then buckled it.

My cheeks felt hot. "Thanks."

"Whatever, punk. Who names their kid Genesis? Hippies?" The man started the car, obviously not wanting a response. Soon we'd left our makeshift parking lot behind and downtown passed by. I hadn't thought to tell him where I lived, and he didn't ask.

"Are you hijacking my car?"

"This piece of crap? Good idea. I bet I can get $200 for it at the junkyard. But I'll have to push you out. Wait, let me speed up."

I laughed, because his sarcasm was obvious. Why couldn't I have met someone like him in high school? I might have stayed. He was snarky and good-looking in the dim light of the car. One of the many reasons I'd left school was because I was different. Not just in seeing things, but in who caught my attention. I'd been beat up half a dozen times, shoved into lockers, even half-drowned in the pool. Most of the time, just being me sucked. Now, sitting in the car, close to a guy who could have been the star of some hit teen miniseries, I was thinking maybe being me wasn't so bad, even if he only spoke to me for a few minutes.

Then there were the other things I saw, like the crazy colors that surrounded people, called auras. Only this guy had no colors—he was just dark. Odd. The darkness still shadowed his eyes in an eerie sort of way. "I can sing for you. Devon says my voice helps chase away the shadows sometimes."

"Who's Devon? Your boyfriend?"

"Lead singer of Wild Park. My band opened for them last night. They've sold a couple million CDs. They're more mainstream than we are, kind of pop. Gotta get your breaks where you can, you know." I paused to study the black edges around his eyes again. "Devon's got shadows too. Like the ones around your eyes." The adrenaline was beginning to wear off. "I don't have a boyfriend at the moment. And my hair is pink 'cause I tried to dye it red, but it didn't work."

"Yeah, the hair screams gay."

"Got a problem with queers? Or are you an asshole to everyone?"

"Only to guys with pink hair who try to run me over."

So, everyone. At least he wasn't a phobe. "I'm sorry. Stuff like this always happens to me."

He raised a brow and glanced my way. "You run people over often?"

"Not that. Just stuff." Between the ghosts, the shadows, and the other crap I saw, something weird was always going on in my life. "I was just trying to get home 'cause I'm tired. Stay away from the shadows and stuff."

"Doesn't everyone have shadows? The whole light-reflection thing?"

"Not the same kind of shadow. Devon's move. His don't like me much. Yours are dark like that too."

"So you see shadows, like a living type of shadow, on me, right now, when there's no light."

"Yeah. Can you see okay? They cover your eyes."

He paused and glanced my way with a strange look on his face. A heavy wave of sleepiness poured over me. "You look tired—you should sleep. You're so not normal. Seeing things that aren't there. You should sleep." The guy's voice faded away abruptly as sleep carried me into vague dreams.

I DON'T know how much time passed before I felt the bed shift beside me and wondered how I'd gotten home. The fact that I obviously wasn't alone didn't seem all that worrisome for some reason. Odd, since I wasn't the kind of guy to bring strangers home, but my brain was a little foggy, so I wasn't concerned.

A warm body curled up beside me, feeling slightly wet, like just from a shower and smelling like the outside after a bad rainstorm. I opened my eyes but just saw a shadowy face in the dark close to mine. The moment was sensual and intimate, even though I couldn't see him clearly.

His lips brushed my cheek, planting small kisses all over my face until finally dipping down to lick at my collarbone. The firm body nestled against mine gave me the confidence to reach forward and touch back. His hair was short, but long enough to grip, and had a slight curl. It felt thicker than most, but product-free and slightly damp. I traced the smooth expanse of his hot, sculpted flesh, while his

10

lips found my mine. He could kiss, and I'd never imagined a kiss could be so sweet.

One of his hands tickled my spine, stroking down my vertebrae as though he were counting them. Each touch made me pull him closer for more contact. It didn't matter that I couldn't see him. His warmth felt good. The closeness so heavenly I couldn't imagine being anywhere else. How long had it been since anyone touched me like I was human and not some freak?

Something in my brain told me we were right together. As the slow torture of warmth built and built, wave upon wave; we rocked against each other like we were all that was left in the world. His arms wrapped so tightly around me I could barely breathe, and that was okay. I could go into the final darkness after a moment like this—let rebirth take me into the next life with one last, amazing memory.

I closed my eyes as his lips found my neck again, this time nipping with a slightly painful sting of teeth. My soul took flight into a blessed state of near unconsciousness.

I wanted to feel him fly away with me, wanted to celebrate the heat of him on my skin and his willingness to hold me. But the encounter seemed to end as quickly as it had begun, leaving me in a waking dream. The loneliness of sleep took me back to where sensual reruns of the encounter circled in many exciting twists.

Kerstrande

IT HAD been an unexpected night. I'd never been hit by a car before, and it had hurt more than I thought it would. A couple of broken ribs and a crack in my skull weren't that big of a deal. My sire had done worse. Those sort of things just took time and blood to heal.

The kid had been easily fooled. Must not know many vampires.

Genesis. Who names their kid after a book in the bible? He couldn't be some sort of religious freak, not with that pink hair,

11

orange jacket, and the purple eye shadow over his large amethyst eyes. Everything about him screamed gay, from the crazy multicolored hair to the bright blue shoes with mini rainbows colored on them.

I'd been out looking for food, only to be rewarded with a fairy pop princess. He sang? Odd, since his voice was pretty deep for a guy so flamboyant. He was probably into techno or some other bullshit.

Felt good, though. Responsive little thing came alive in my arms and never pushed me away once. Even when I bit him. And sweet Jesus, he had tasted like heaven.

I drank a little too long. Should have pulled away sooner. But how long had it been since I'd actually enjoyed a feeding? In fact, had I ever before?

Anya's bloody, lifeless eyes flashed through my memory. Yeah, I'd never enjoyed it before. Just because I was a monster didn't mean I had to like playing the part. I had to eat to live. I got that. Had it ingrained the hard way, unfortunately, but still hadn't made peace with it.

Only now, while I watched the kid, hoping his fast breathing would even out, I realized that maybe, just maybe, there was more to being a vampire. Maybe I had to drink from flaming musicians to satisfy the craving. If they all gave me peace like this one had, I'd stalk a whole city of them. I could read the headlines now, probably write them myself: "Pretty Queer Boys Everywhere Run Scared from Vampire Stalker."

I laughed to myself, wondering where the levity had come from. The kid's breath settled, and he fell off into REM sleep. Maybe I'd given him a good dream or two, even if he'd only been half awake. Now that he seemed to be safely sleeping and not dead, I lay back to let myself drift off, thanking my fortune for an easy meal and the first company in months.

CHAPTER 2

Genesis

THE sun raged through an open window with a glare powerful enough to rouse the dead. I expected to wake in my own bed or even my car. Instead, I stared at an unfamiliar ceiling from my spot in a large, really firm mattress. A thick, blue blanket wrapped me up like a sausage. It had the earthy smell of a summer night after a rainstorm. Thankfully, the room appeared to be absent of all nonliving types. And for the first time in months, I actually felt rested.

Memories of the dream repeated in my head. Had it been a dream? It felt so real, but my dreams were often that way. If it hadn't been a dream, the encounter must have been with the guy I hit with my car. What little I'd seen of him had been beautiful, minus all the bruises and cuts from a car accident, of course. The idea of touching him again, having him hold me, made the sleepiness disappear pretty quickly. Dream or not, I'd remember it for a while for sure.

From beyond the partially open doorway to the left, the sound of a gurgling coffeepot drew me from the comfortable bed. Coffee seasoned the air with a heavenly scent. I followed my nose—happy to see I was still dressed, even if my clothes were rumpled—to the

13

kitchen, where the victim of my haphazard driving leaned against the counter.

Something about the way he stood, or maybe it was the fake light of the kitchen's hanging lamps, made him look familiar. He was good-looking in a Nordic-plus-something-much-more-foreign way. Like a European pop star might be. His hair was a strong gold-blond color with red highlights, giving it a copperish glow. His eyes were a pale brown, unshadowed this morning. He was tall, probably around six feet, broad shouldered, long-legged, face a little angular and sharp. His clothes were not something off a rack, and the kitchen was high-end, granite counters and stainless steel. He came from money or was money. It was all the same anyway. Yet I felt like I'd met him years ago and was finally reunited with an old friend or lover. He couldn't have been older than eighteen or nineteen, but he stood like a man twice our age, heavy, as though the weight of the world lay on his shoulders.

"Stare much?" The snark was back.

I had to peel my gaze away from the charcoal-gray sweater that hugged his arms to look up into his stormy amber-colored eyes. "Thanks for letting me sleep and all that." I crossed the room to lean against the counter beside him. The dream I'd had last night made heat rise in my cheeks. Had I been dreaming of him? Would a guy like this really kiss me? I could imagine those arms wrapped around me, his lips on mine.

"Your shadows are gone—that's good." I looked around the stylish condo; yeah, he had money all right. Leather furniture, big screen TV.... I was so out of my league. At least the place was absent of Preservation Group paraphernalia. Did he live with someone? Maybe an older lover who paid for a sweet place like this? "I don't remember getting here or anything." The memory of nearly having an out-of-body experience made me shudder. Maybe it hadn't been a dream. "Did we do anything?"

"Do?"

"You and I didn't...."

EVOLUTION

"Does your ass hurt?" He growled at something he must have seen on my face, though the sound of that low rumble had heat rising to my cheeks. I shifted, hoping he wouldn't notice I was probably beet red. "You're not girly enough for me."

Yet he gave off body language that said otherwise. He stood close enough for me to lean forward if I wanted. I guess that's why people instantly know I'm queer. Can't stop from looking at what I like. Instead, I picked at invisible lint on my hoodie. "Nice place… yours?"

"No. I randomly break into other people's apartments to abuse young men with pink hair and use the coffeemaker." His sarcastic humor made me smile. He poured two cups of steaming brown liquid and added cream and sugar to both. He looked peaceful for a whole thirty seconds as he took that first sip. His eyes flicked to the second mug, and I wasted no time sucking down the wonderful brew. Real coffee, sweet Buddha. I'd been drinking the stuff since I was eleven, my mom telling me the whole time it would stunt my growth. The truth was that being Asian made me short, not drinking coffee, and I was pretty okay with that.

"Have we met before?" I finally asked, thinking I probably would have remembered meeting a guy like him before. He hadn't gone to my high school, but there had been many schools in the area. Maybe I'd seen him at a show somewhere. Was he in the scene? He had the hands of an artist, which was broad enough to mean he could be a musician.

"Other than when you hit me with your car? No. And that's an encounter I'd rather not repeat."

"But I've seen you somewhere before." Maybe he'd been to Down Low, the gay dance club where I waited tables. I wasn't legally supposed to be working at the Down Low, since I was underage. But I'd be eighteen in a few months, and the cops rarely showed. When they did, I knew how to get the hell out. I brushed my hair back; it was probably a nest by now, but I couldn't take my eyes off him. He was so beautiful.

There were plenty of guys who came through the club every night. After a while, they all started to look the same. Just more random guys, some hot, some not, who were looking for a hookup without complications. I'd met more than my fair share of "daddies" who wanted to take care of me. My friend Cris often encouraged me to find someone, said I was too young to be on my own. But I did okay, and Cris wasn't one to talk since he was barely nineteen himself, and he'd lived on his own forever.

"I've just got one of those faces." He proceeded into the living room with his cup in hand. "You should eat something. There are eggs in the fridge. The protein would be good for you."

I wasn't hungry, and the offer seemed a little odd. "Ever go to Down Low?" I asked, adding a touch more cream to my coffee.

"I'm not gay." Yet he knew of the club, obviously.

I sighed and gulped down the rest of my brew before rinsing the mug and putting it in the dishwasher. No need for me to make a mess. The one thing I'd learned pretty fast about making my own way was there was no one else to clean up after me, ever.

I followed him into the living room, only to pause in the doorway. Frames decorated the walls behind the massive sofa: gold records, album covers, and autographed pictures. A Grammy perched on the shelf in the corner. The reality hit me like one of those cartoon safes.

"You're from Triple Flight. Lead guitarist, Kerstrande Petterson." Rock god, guitar genius, and heartthrob to millions. TF had traveled the world a few times. I'd even seen them in concert, always stuck in back where the cheapest tickets were, but I'd been there. Five years ago they'd been the youngest rock band to ever grace the cover of *Rolling Stone*. Kerstrande didn't look any different than he had the last time I saw him on TV.

"Just figured that out now?"

Again I felt stuck, like I had in the car last night when I'd hit him. Heart pounding, body frozen, mind racing. We were ruined. Evolution was over. Sure, we'd never had the musical genius of

Triple Flight. Not been signed by the age of fifteen and billionaires by the age of eighteen, but we were good. We were real.

"Are you crying?"

I brought my hand up to my face and felt the warmth of tears. Sure enough. First I hit the guy with my car then I make a fool of myself by crying like a baby in front of him. "No," I denied it.

An uncomfortable silence filled the room until he said, "So you're in a band."

"I'm sorry. Please don't ruin us. We're just starting out. Making our own album and everything. Robert and Joel didn't do anything. I'll just quit, let them find a new singer. It's not their fault. This is their dream...." Mine too, even more so than theirs. But I would give it up for my friends. After all, it had been my mistake.

"Decent singers are hard to find."

A dime a dozen, really. I'd auditioned for a couple hundred bands before Rob and I had formed our own. Kerstrande stared at me like he didn't know what to make of me. "Making your own record? You probably won't sell more than one or two thousand copies. The big companies have the dollars for promotion—that's what all bands need. Is that what you're here for? Promotion? Call the press, make it happen."

"You think I planned this? Do people try to run you over often?"

"No. That's new."

Yet not. His snarky attitude said it all. He expected people to take advantage of him. The humor was a shield. I got that, since I used the same cover myself sometimes, but I wasn't looking for anything. "Do I seem the type?"

"Everyone's the type, kid. Everyone wants fame, fortune, and power. What they don't get is that getting all that puts you in a fishbowl. No one is really your friend, and no one wants you for you. Merry Christmas. Santa Claus isn't real."

I sighed. "I don't want fame, power, and fortune. I'd like to have enough money to eat and keep a roof over my head, but I sing because I love to sing. I want people to smile, maybe even escape from their pain for a little while. I didn't know who you were until I came into this room. Sorry I interrupted your self-pity party." I turned toward the kitchen, hoping I could find my keys so I could get the hell out. I felt bad for the guy, but not enough to let him dink me around. I'd left school and my old neighborhood because of guys like him and was so done with that. Guys who were bullies just 'cause it made them feel important. "Where are my keys?"

His eyes met mine, and we shared a glare. He was the first to look away. "You're right. You're not smart enough to have done this on purpose."

Okay, now he was going too far. "At least I'm not a conceited prick who needs to flaunt money and pay people to be his friends. Where are my keys?"

"Better a prick than a sociopath."

Was he having fun with the banter? Did no one talk back to him? What the hell? "Seriously, I already told you I didn't do it on purpose." Just because he was Kerstrande Petterson didn't give him the right to be a jerk. I frowned, remembering something he'd said last night. "And who are you to make fun of my name when your name is so weird?"

He blinked and said nothing for a few seconds. "I get it. You're schizophrenic, right?"

"Only if I can change the meaning of schizophrenia to being really pissed off that you won't give me my keys!" I was so done with this conversation.

He threw the keys at my feet. "Get out. I've had enough of that cotton candy hair of yours."

"Gladly." I scooped them up and headed for the door. When it closed behind me and I headed toward the parking lot outside, I felt momentarily lost, like I should go back, apologize, and try to get him to see that I wasn't after him for money. But just like all things in life,

EVOLUTION

I had to keep moving forward. The only person's view on the world you could change was your own. Everyone else had to make their own damn decisions.

My car looked dented and slightly battered. I knew how it felt. At least it still ran. After a quick trip home, I fed my cat Mikka, who just glared at me like I'd been neglecting her. I changed into work clothes, skimpy, tight, and see-through, and cleaned up my raccoon eyes. Some of the waiters wore only hot pants, but I'd had too many hands on me to suffer not having something between them and me.

It was early enough in the day that the worst of the crowd hadn't arrived yet. Mostly it was people just stopping in for an early dinner. Even my bandmate, Rob, who was as straight as guys got, came in for a soda and some food. He sat in my section, watching whatever sports game played on the big screen. He shared his food with me while I cleaned around him and waited on the few people who lingered near the bar. The music, barely at a dull throb, let me tell Rob about my encounter with Kerstrande Petterson. I left out the dream, since Rob often freaked when I went into too much detail about my sex life.

"I'm surprised it's not on the news." He took a sip of his soda and flipped his long rock-star-esque hair out of his eyes. He always wore tight jeans and leather, hair almost screaming eighties; I'd seen the pictures in his mom's high school yearbook. But there wasn't much I could say since mine was skater punk on neon steroids.

"They broke up years ago." I remember sobbing over the last release in memorial to their greatness. I'd been fifteen at the time.

"Still, he's local. Seems like anytime some local celeb farts, we know about it."

Someone squeezed passed me and then slapped my butt before sitting down at Rob's table. It was Joel, our keyboardist. He winked at me, not at all bothered by the half-naked men dancing in cages this early in the evening. Rob always went out of his way to look away from them. Joel played both sides of the fence, so he looked his fill. "Hey, rock star. You should flip the TV to channel ten."

My heart skipped a beat, but I went for the remote and changed the station.

"Former guitarist Kerstrande Petterson caught on tape with a young man. Are they lovers? You decide." The picture posted on the screen was a dark blurry image of him carrying me in a fireman's grip up to his apartment. That explained why my stomach ached today. I'd bounced on his shoulder like a sack of potatoes. "The New York native has refused all comments, and we are still searching for the identity of the young man."

"Damn," I mumbled.

Rob's eyes, large as saucers, stared at the news. Had he not believed me before?

Joel grinned. "I totally agree. You've been holding out on us. Shacking up with a rock demigod. He owns half of REA Records now. You can't do better than Petterson to help Evolution."

"I hit him with my car. It was an accident. I don't want anything from him." Especially after the talk I'd had with him that morning.

"He looks fine in the photos. Maybe he's seen you here a few times and was playing hurt to get you to go home with him."

"It's not like that." Besides, I wasn't going to hang onto the guy for his fame, money, or other crap. I was old enough to make my own way in the world. Just working at Down Low provided me with plenty of opportunities for sugar daddies. But getting paid to spread wasn't the way I lived and sure as hell not how I worked.

The evening crowd started to file in, and my friends left. I let the work take my mind off the events from last night. Petterson would forget about me soon enough anyway, and I'd forget him. Maybe.

I danced to the music, sung along to some of my favorite tunes, and winked at a ton of drooling daddies who piled in after the workday ended for most. More than a handful of men had their hands on me as the evening progressed. I shrugged them all off, thinking only of the stranger in my dreams who had held me so tightly. It couldn't have been Petterson. He wasn't nice enough to hold anyone that way.

When I finally got home to my studio apartment, it was after 2:00 a.m., and I dragged myself to the microwave to watch the Styrofoam box spin. The best thing about having a small place was that I never had far to go. Not for food, to the bathroom, or to sleep.

I stripped out of my shirt and dug into the food while perched on the edge of my futon. A spot just above my left collarbone had been bothering me all day. Either a really big spider had gotten me at Kerstrande's or he'd given me a hickey. My brain kept going back to the memory of the nip of teeth. If I had to endure another bite to experience more of those kisses, I'd be all over it.

Tossing the food aside, I kicked off my pants and pulled a blanket up, wondering if I'd dream of him again. The phone rang. Who the hell called this late at night? Had my mom had some sort of emergency? I picked up the phone. "Hello?"

"Genesis Sage? This is Five Live News calling. What is your relationship with Kerstrande Petterson? Are you business partners? Lovers? Are you the reason he gave up stardom? Does he feel that Triple Flight would lose popularity if he came out?"

I hung up the phone, feeling the fear of the fishbowl closing in on me. Obviously they'd found me. Someone buzzed the call box from downstairs. "Genesis Sage, are you home? This is Ten News. We'd like to ask you some questions." I turned off the phone, trembling a little. They'd have to ask Kerstrande if they wanted answers. It was his fishbowl, not mine, and I didn't want to swim.

CHAPTER 3

FOUR days of dodging the media and another four hours of rehearsing with Devon's supervision left me feeling like I had been sucked up in a vacuum, spun around, and spit into the trash. Joel and Rob handled the criticism better than I. Devon had a cruel streak when it came to me. Sometimes I feared it was because I'd never taken him up on his many offers for activities outside of work, but *friend* was all he was to me.

Since the picture turned up of me with Kerstrande, we'd had hundreds of requests to perform a headlining show. We'd turned most down. Our manager booked us at Hard Light, the biggest indie club in the city. No opening act, just Evolution in front of a million cameras. Joel said it was standing room only. I doubted anyone really wanted to hear me sing. They just wanted to stare at the freak who had been caught with an ex-rock star.

Devon sipped lemon water and put his feet on the table, stretching out like a lazy cat. Always the predator, whether he was singing, dating, or just existing. He projected that sense of extreme confidence, much like a business shark. His shadows swirled around him tonight, live and hungry-looking. The past few weeks he'd grown worse. More critical, darker, and sometimes downright scary.

"Bad press can be turned into good press."

EVOLUTION

"How can I turn this into something good? They don't want me. They want some sideshow." I pulled on black leather pants and a white wife beater. All the lights would make me sweat like a pig, but I'd try to keep it as cool as I could. Rob had asked me to tone down the color for the night, and I promised I would. In fact, other than my hair, my blue rainbow shoes were the only color they would see on me tonight. Even my nails were painted black. I could be butch too. Well, sorta.

"Be you," Devon told me. "I like you just fine the way you are."

I sighed at him. "If only life were that easy." The fact that Hard Light had about a half dozen ghosts, one of which was putting a gun in his mouth over and over again just ten feet from where Devon sat, made my anxiety rise. I really hoped the stage was clean. No need to give the guys more reasons to stare at me like I was crazy.

Joel fidgeted with a candy bar. "I've never seen this much press in one place. You'd think we were new recruits of the NFL or something." Joel looked like he could have been in the NFL; he was sort of stocky, so it made sense why people didn't bug him like they did me. He could play gay really well, lisp and limp wrist and swish his hips, but he liked girls too much to ever commit to one guy.

Rob pulled his long hair back into a ponytail. "We're good. We deserve this break. Just remember, we're Evolution."

"Um, sure," I grumbled. "Don't you guys think getting all this attention 'cause I hit a rock star with my car is a bad thing?" Like bad Karma adding up to some catastrophe I couldn't yet see. I'd ridden the subway tonight, hiding—hood up, dark shades covering half my face, and praying no one pointed and shouted, "Hey, it's him!"

"Best thing that could have happened to us." Joel handed me the candy bar. I dropped it into my bag, since chocolate made my throat funny.

The buzz of the media flowed louder from the other side of the backstage door. "Mr. Petterson. Mr. Petterson!" The blood in my head drained to my feet. *He* was here. He wasn't supposed to remember I existed anymore.

Rob opened the door with a frown. Kerstrande walked in, shut the door, and leaned against it. He looked like the star he was in tan pants, white dress shirt, and a light sport coat. Even Devon looked ordinary next to him.

Devon growled at Kerstrande. I looked back at my mentor and wondered what was up. "No wonder you're so hot for Genesis. Let me tell you now, he's not in your league."

"Saxon" was Kerstrande's only acknowledgment of Devon. Did they know each other? Petterson's glare was all for me. He took a step toward me.

I stepped back, worried by the violent promise in his eyes. Did he want to kiss me or hit me? "I didn't tell them anything."

"And *that* is the problem!" He yanked me out the door into the brigade of photographers. Within seconds, my sight was lost to pops of colorless spots from all the flashes. Questions flew from all directions. Kerstrande ignored them all and addressed the microphones. "I'd like everyone to meet my new creative project. Genesis Sage of Evolution. Evolution's debut will be produced under the REA label by nothing but the best producers and songwriters. I think you'll find that though they have a different sound than Triple Flight, they are just as talented."

I felt like a gaping fish in the spotlight. How could REA produce us if we hadn't signed anything? Kerstrande had never even heard us play. We had a handful of live shows up on YouTube, but nothing of good quality.

He breezed through a couple dozen questions with cool finesse. I couldn't remember most of them since my mind was too busy trying to keep up with the endless tide of my own. "If you'll excuse us, ladies and gentlemen, Evolution will be performing now."

Kerstrande had to drag me to the edge of the stage where Rob and Joel waited. They both stood openmouthed with shock, but otherwise ready to play.

"You better be good, punk, or your career is over."

EVOLUTION

He pushed me toward my friends and disappeared into the darkness behind the stage. Tonight, the idea of performing brought a strong sense of dread and terror. Damn. I'd been singing in public since I could stand. No one was getting the better of me. Not when it came to music. Was I, or was I not, a pro?

I took a deep breath and stepped up to the florescent marker tape on the floor. Someone hooked a replay-phone in my ear so I could hear myself sing, and I wished I'd had more time to practice. *Shake it off, Genesis*, I scolded myself. *You can do this.*

The lights came up. Joel began the keyboard melody and synthesized drumbeat that rolled us flawlessly into a heavy rock-pop sound. Rob and I stared in mutual horror at the crowd. A few cameras were actually a couple thousand, including several large TV stations. People crammed into rows all the way up into the rarely used balcony.

Rob shrugged and poured himself into the guitar opening right on Joel's cue. Seven seconds later, my turn came, and surprisingly, my voice worked well enough to get the upbeat song going. In thirty seconds the nervousness wore off and all that mattered was the music. My voice carried the passion I had for singing and the many hours a day I practiced. I sank into the rhythm, using the deep sound to wrap the words in emotion and change the crowd's energy. Their auras changed colors from apprehensive red/brown to gleeful white, gold, and orange, a fall rainbow that lifted my spirit too.

Nearly two hours I sang without more than a few seconds break. Onstage, I wasn't much of a talker. But I laughed with the crowd at Joel and Rob's antics, danced to our crazy music, and sang with everything I had. When we finally stepped off the stage, we'd played three encores and every original song we'd ever practiced. I was so tired I nearly had to crawl to the dressing room.

The white top had been lost onstage halfway through. The sweat dripped from my hair, sending a shiver down my shoulders. Hard Light didn't have personal dressing rooms with showers like some of the larger venues Devon played. Sadly, he stayed around anyway. And from the shadows that lingered in the hall outside the room, something bothered him in a big way.

"The crowd warmed up to you fairly quickly." He still sat in the chair, his silhouette outlined by the light from the doorway. The lights were off and the room felt like a meat locker, cold enough to see my breath. This side of Devon I didn't want to confront, mostly because I wasn't sure it *was* Devon at all. "You'll find yourself well received by the press now."

I stared in his direction, feeling his anger and jealousy from across the room. I didn't know what emotion worked best at that moment. Returning his irritation would be easiest, but not if I wanted us to remain friends. My friend, rival, mentor, and tormentor needed help. But I was pretty sure he wouldn't let me help him. There was a time when he was the big brother of my heart. I told him everything, and his easy smile had helped me get through some of the hardest things in my life, like dropping out of school and finding my way on my own. Only in the past few months had he really begun to change. Now he rarely smiled, and I didn't feel like I could tell him anything. Had the darkness within him pushed us so far apart?

"You'll have a good chance with REA. They'll market you right."

The label meant nothing to me. He knew that. "What's wrong, Devon? Why are you so dark tonight?" The few years he had on me felt like a million at that moment.

Without my even seeing him move, he suddenly stood before me, his hand on my face feeling like ice. My breathing was shallow, fear etching a strong presence in my head. Even my peculiarities were child's play next to Devon's.

"Please tell me what's wrong. I want to help."

He stepped away, his body shaking. The cold rolled off him in waves. "You can't help. Sorry, Gene." He left, taking the oppressive feeling of the shadows with him. I frowned at his back, watching him step out of my life again. The two years I'd known him felt so short when he kept vanishing into the darkness. He'd been doing that a lot lately.

Kerstrande entered the room while I was drying my hair. He shut the door firmly behind him and leaned against it. Rob and Joel were packing up their instruments and would be back soon. The dim cast of the digital clock was the only light in the room. "You write those songs?"

"Yeah."

"Gibberish. That voice is wasted by your lack of polish."

Had there been a compliment in there? "You like my voice?"

He flicked on the light, ignoring my question. "Why are you sitting in the dark?"

"I'm just drying my hair. I don't need light for that." If I'd been able to get the pants off I'd probably have been naked when he walked in, but I didn't share that.

"Do you always strip on stage or was that just for the billion cameras?"

"I was hot!"

"And ten more minutes and the pants would have come off." He sounded jealous.

I blinked at him—could he read minds or something? "They're stuck. I can't get them off." That's why I normally wore jeans and left the leather to Devon, but he'd insisted I wear them tonight.

Color flushed Kerstrande's cheeks. He stared at me for a few seconds before yanking his sport coat off and putting it around my shoulders. "Let's go. I'll give you a ride home."

"My home or yours?" The way he leaned toward me and touched my shoulders made me wonder if he liked me, or was I really just his creative project like he told the reporters? Unlike Devon, Kerstrande's emotions were buried deep. His darkness was more internal, a wall to protect himself against others. How hard would it be to breach that barrier? The more important question was: would he push me away if I tried?

I stepped in close, letting my fingers caress his arm. He stared at them, a mix of hope and fear on his face. "The press have found my place. But we can sneak around them if you'd like to come home with

27

me for a while." The innuendo was clear, and by the look on his face, Kerstrande wanted to take me up on it. A moment later he shook it off and his expression was neutral again. He towered over me, eyes still shadow-free. Maybe the darkness only chased Devon tonight.

"I told you my singing helped. You have no shadows." I touched his face, loving the feel of him beneath my hands. He didn't flinch away either. Instead, he raised his hand; fingers lightly brushed my neck, lingering on the spot that was slowly healing since it'd appeared after being in his house.

"I think you imagined them the other night."

"Hmm."

Someone knocked on the door before entering a second later. Rob looked shocked and irritated to see Kerstrande touching me and me touching him. "What's going on?"

I stepped away, irritated that I felt guilty, and Kerstrande dropped his hand. He moved toward the doorway. "I'm going to give your pop prince a ride home."

Rob wasn't ready to let it go. "You did all this. We haven't signed anything with you. The media is after us because of you. Then you put Gene out there with no support other than his band. It's like you wanted him to fail. What the hell is your problem?"

"The only support you'll ever get is what your band provides. Everyone else is just out to screw you. Learn the hard lessons now and it won't hurt so much later." Kerstrande took my hand and yanked me toward the door.

Rob grabbed my free arm. "You're not a dog, Gene. You don't have to follow when he says so or put up with his insults. I'll give you a ride home. I'm surprised Devon didn't stick around to take you home."

I didn't want to go with Rob or Devon. Kerstrande made my heart pound; his expression said he didn't care, but his body was turned in my direction, stance saying it was ready to defend. He wanted me to come with him, even if he wasn't ready to shout it to the world yet, even if he didn't understand what that meant.

"It's okay, Rob. It's just a ride. We'll be talking shop." Whatever made it easier for Rob to accept. I worried that someday I'd cross the line, and we'd end the delicate balance that allowed us to be friends. But not tonight.

Joel appeared in the doorway. He stuffed chips into my bag as Kerstrande and I passed. "Night, kiddo. Don't forget the safeword." He winked at us. Kerstrande's grip on my hand tightened.

The parking lot echoed with crickets, but no press, thankfully. Kerstrande's Mercedes put Joel's Mustang to shame. I got in and sucked in the scent of new leather, smoke, and Kerstrande.

"Your place," he said.

"Okay." I gave him the address. His frown grew. Was he worried about my neighborhood?

He reached over and snapped the seat belt into place. I studied my hands to keep from looking at him and acting like a fool. "Thanks, sorry."

He said nothing, just started the car and then off we went. The car drove like a dream, smooth, fast, but silent. Why didn't he listen to music? The Honda's radio was broken, but in a car this nice the speaker system could probably rival something from a movie theater. I imagined Michael Shuon, lead singer of Triple Flight, singing "Red Rose," his voice streaming in surround sound, guitar all moody behind him.

Neither of us said anything for the whole ride. Kerstrande kept a neutral expression while we made our way upstairs. I knew it wasn't the glamorous place like he had. He had closets bigger than my studio. But he didn't say or do anything to indicate it bothered him.

"Sorry," I told him once we were inside. "I don't come from money like Rob or Joel. So I just get by on the money I make at Down Low." I went behind the screen, kept just for occasions my sister came over, and wriggled out of the pants to pull on a pair of loose-fitting boxers. When I came back out, Kerstrande was staring at a picture of my mom and my sister and I. "Mom sends me a little each month to help, and Uo makes me food all the time."

"Uo?"

"My sister."

"Who names their kid Uo?"

"Grandpa named us both. He teaches at a temple in northern New York."

"Jewish?"

"Buddhist."

He just seemed to absorb the knowledge. At least he wasn't griping about my religion yet. "How'd you get Genesis and she got Uo?"

Because I'd changed my name years ago to something I felt fit me better. "Guess I just got the luck of the draw."

He glanced out the single window, which was a great view of the brick building two feet away. "So why didn't you just stay with your family? You're a kid, no one would care."

"I dropped out. Just couldn't handle all the noise and trouble of school. I passed the GED, but just barely. Mom couldn't afford to keep supporting me, and I didn't want to burden Uo or Grandpa." Not to mention my coming out had kind of alienated me from my old neighborhood. "I do all right on my own."

He nosed through cupboards, most of which were empty. "On ramen noodles and the junk food your friend gives you?" He opened the fridge and stared at the barren shelves. I had lots of condiments, but that was about it. "No beer?"

"I'm underage." Not like I had money for booze anyway. Water was free. "I'll be eighteen in a few months, though. Are you legal?" He didn't look a day older than eighteen, but maybe the rich and famous didn't care about the law.

He swore silently, then shut the fridge and plopped down heavily on the futon. The old metal frame groaned in response to his added weight. When was the last time I'd brought someone home? Never, probably; that took trust.

I sat down beside him, wrapped my arms around my legs, and waited for him to decide which direction the evening was going to go.

More shop? Or something else? He slid closer and brushed the hair out of my eyes with his fingers. He seemed so lost in the moment. I just waited until his lips touched mine and opened for him. When his tongue slipped in to duel with mine, I pressed back, tasting him further. I let my mind clear of everything but thoughts of him—none of which were G-rated.

He tickled my hip, caressing the skin with the pads of his fingers, swirling his thumb just below the top of my shorts. I sucked on his lower lip, he moved to recapture mine, and it became a fierce game. It didn't matter that I was turned on, and he likely was too. What mattered was the time we spent locked together like that, just enjoying the taste of each other, the quiet companionship and acceptance.

Finally, he let the kisses fall away and rested his forehead against mine. With those amber eyes so close, lashes thick and full shading them, he looked beautiful and so terribly young. In that moment, we could have been peers in so many more ways, even though he had money and power and I was just a dropout from nowhere. I touched his face, stroked his cheek, and just breathed his breath for a while. We probably could have stared for hours.

Unfortunately, the paper-thin door brought the sounds of voices in the hall. Reporters. Someone probably opened the downstairs door for them.

Kerstrande's personal wall came back up like it'd been resurrected with instant concrete. He growled at the door before turning back to me. His lips brushed mine again for a few seconds before he swept himself away. "Another time, brat."

He was gone before I had a chance to move. After I locked the door and dimmed the lights, all I could think of was the way his lips felt on mine. I'd never felt so connected to anyone before. Certainly not the handful of guys I'd had as lovers. My body felt sated, calm, and happy. I sighed and lay back on the futon, letting myself replay the kiss in my head as sleep took me away to dream of his amber-colored eyes.

CHAPTER 4

Kerstrande

YOU'D think after years of dodging the media, one would become a pro at it. Sadly, the time made them bolder and more persistent, and me, just more irritated. My head was too full of Gene to have enough capacity left to sort out reasonably intelligent lies to tell the scavengers. I brushed passed them all, went down to my car, and then headed out to the open road.

Gene's talk of shadows infuriated me, mostly because I was pretty sure he was telling the truth. How much could I have escaped if only I'd seen them myself years ago? And oh, how his voice made me miss those old days. Back when I was truly young and innocent just like him. The music made me fly and nothing mattered but the song. He'd been right about it chasing the anger away. Whether it was really the sound of his voice or the pure, clear, magic-like innocence that poured free into his song, I didn't know. Guess it really didn't matter.

I parked in the underground lot of my building. Nothing else interested me tonight. I still felt the lingering heat of his lips, almost like a ghost. Would I ruin him if I went back for more? Everything else turned to crap. Triple Flight, Anya, life in general. Who knew signing a contract to become the next big musician at the age of fifteen would result in messing up my life so much?

A note pinned to my door with a knife brought the reality back down.

Apparently New York didn't have room for one more monster. A map of the city, lines redrawn, told me I had to leave. Damn territorial bastard. Years of closely drawn alliances erased. Major players were missing. Was he whittling down the competition?

One vampire couldn't handle a city this size on his own. Not even the King.

I'd play by his rules for now. Moving didn't mean I had to leave altogether. The Park was still neutral ground, hunting grounds. And there were other pieces in play that interested me more, as the taste of incense and rain still clung to my lips.

Genesis

THE next few days were a whirlwind of contract negotiations and working at the club. I spent every spare moment of thought dreaming about Kerstrande's kiss. I'd even looked him up online to try to get more information. Though just like his sarcastic personality projected, he didn't share much with anyone.

On the third day, I dressed nice, left my hair in a seminormal color of red-brown, and made my way to Kerstrande's apartment. He'd commented he didn't like the liner and glitter, but I felt naked without something on my face, so I'd kept the liner light and used an almost nude shadow. It gave my eyes depth. Maybe Kerstrande would like it.

I knocked on his door, hoping to throw myself at him. Maybe he'd let me kiss him again.

The fact that the reporters had vanished from their camp around his building and mine proved his deception had worked. I'd been signed less than a day, and already the world had lost interest. For that I was more than a little thankful.

I knocked again when there was no answer. A cold chill ran down my spine, alerting me to the fact I wasn't alone in the hallway anymore.

"He's gone," a female voice told me. She sounded ragged and tired, almost like a recording that was fading. Sometimes when a ghost was around for a while, they got that way.

"Who's gone?" I asked without looking back. However she'd died, I didn't need to see. The ones who lingered almost always kept their appearance at death because they couldn't understand that last moment.

"The musician. Moved out before sunup yesterday."

My heart skipped a beat. He'd moved and not said anything to me?

"That one's haunted. Lots of ghosts."

I took a deep breath. "Thanks." My feet took me back to the car while I willed myself not to look back. The sky was dark, reminding me that it was my only night off this week. I should have been at home resting, but on the way I had to stop.

Central Park stood a long barrier between his home and the longer journey to mine. I wiped back the tears, ignored a handful of otherworldly clingers, and got a chili-cheese dog from the vender near the parking lot. Usually my favorite food, the treat tasted a bit like cardboard as I thought about maybe never seeing Kerstrande again. We had something together, more than just a kiss.

"You actually look normal. I barely recognized you without the circus hair and headlights glaring down at me." The voice made me swallow wrong and choke. Kerstrande towered over me, looking amused and irritated all at once.

I felt like I was hacking up a hairball for a good two minutes before I could talk. "You scared me."

He touched my hair, fingers tickling my scalp as they ran through the length.

"Do you like it?" Maybe he just didn't like the flamboyant side of me.

"No." He sat down and lit a smoke.

I sighed, not sure how to read him right now. "You moved."

"Yeah, had to get away from the stalkers."

Like the press, or me? I didn't ask what I didn't want to know. "We signed the contracts today. I wonder if it will be that crazy for us." I just wanted to sing. The whole fame thing was not a bonus. Not seeing dead people would be nice, but no piece of paper could take that away.

We sat in silence for a bit. He'd already made his stance on the music business clear, so I wasn't going to push it, even if he owned half the label. At least our time together didn't feel awkward. "So is Kerstrande your real name?" I finally asked.

"Yes. Kerstrande Charleston Petterson. What a load of crap, right?"

I smiled. He had no idea how bad it could be. "KC."

"Huh?"

"Your initials are KC, sounds like Casey." I liked it. Simple and uncomplicated. He didn't answer, which I took to mean he either didn't mind or would snark at me later. "I didn't expect to see you here tonight."

"Temporary lapse in judgment. Maybe I should get that lobotomy scheduled after all." He rose from the bench, flicked away his old cigarette, and lit a new one on his way to the parking lot.

I jumped up to follow, rushed to keep up with him, and then matched his stride. "Can we talk?"

"I'm not much of a talker."

"Why are you running away? Don't you like me?"

"I don't know what you're talking about." He still moved toward his car and away from me.

"Why did you kiss me?"

"Temporary lapse in judgment."

"Didn't you like it?" Didn't he feel the connection I had? He was so far out of my league I almost didn't dare to look. But he had paused, eyes lost in the dark, staring in the opposite direction.

"You should go home. The Park isn't safe at night."

I stepped up beside him and grabbed his hand, massaging his palm with my thumb. "Can't you tell it to me straight?"

"I'm not gay."

"I'm not asking you to be. I'm just asking you to be you. The you who kissed me." The him that accepted me for who I was.

Again we stood in silence for a while, only the crickets chirping around us. He curled his fingers in my hair, face close, unguarded for the moment, looking so vulnerable. When his lips brushed mine, wariness clouded his face. The shadows around his eyes grew, gathering like some dark mass in a horror movie. "Just for tonight," he whispered almost more to himself than me.

"Okay," I told him.

He turned back toward the parking lot with me following close behind. The car we approached was a black BMW sports car. It was pretty, flashy, and probably worth more than I'd make in my lifetime. "I ditched the Mercedes. Paparazzi kept tabs on my plates."

I nodded as though I understood the disposal of expensive cars. He deactivated the alarm and unlocked the doors. I got into the passenger seat feeling like I should have maybe put plastic over the leather or something to keep from messing it up. He slid in, reached over, and snapped my seat belt into place.

That was all I remembered of the drive.

The shadows took over, stealing consciousness from me for a while. Landmarks blended into dark blotches, and the world faded.

Rob had gotten me drunk once. I'd passed out, been sick for days afterward. This felt like that, only magnified. Like I was floating in a smoky cloud of uncertainty. The car stopped while I sat on the verge of an abyss.

Kerstrande appeared beside my door, opened it, and unbuckled the belt. "Coming?" His hand stretched toward me engulfed in dark goo. I gripped the metal of the car, pressed cold beneath my fingers. Nothing else felt real. His skin was warm but not solid, more molasses and fading memories than corporal.

"I feel really weird."

"Weird how?" He wrapped his arm around my waist, holding me up, and led me toward a door. "You change your mind?"

"No." But it took several attempts to get the word out.

The door opened to an ordinary hotel room: large bed, brownish-red covers, tan walls, nature art. It all seemed to spin around me. He helped me to the bed, where I fell back and stared at the ceiling.

His jacket rustled, the only noise in the room besides my pounding heart and ragged breath. I watched him unbutton his shirt with a semidetached feeling. He stood molded out of shadows and haze. My brain tried to pull the images out of the taffy-clogged edges, but succeeded only in tiring me even further.

"I feel fuzzy." Like my limbs were falling asleep, needles piercing in the thousands throughout my whole body.

"It'll pass." He leaned over me now, unbuttoning the nice shirt I'd worn just for him, and trailed an icy path over my skin with his fingertips.

"You're cold. Are you sick, KC?"

"I'll be warm soon. Do you want this?"

"Yes, but I'm really fuzzy."

"Fuzzy how? Did you drink something? I don't smell alcohol."

"I never drink." Not since that awful first time when I was sixteen.

After a pause, he brushed the crotch of my pants. I sighed and tried to arch my hips into his touch.

"You seem happy."

"It's nice." Maybe I was more than a little loopy too.

"Just nice?"

"I'm pretty fuzzy." Like a TV out of focus, my brain cast snow around the room, freezing the image briefly before letting it come back into motion again.

"Do you want me or not?" He sounded frustrated.

"Yes, please." I smiled, looking up into what I thought was his face, though it was all one big shadow. I'd give anything for him to wrap his arms around me again. "If you want."

"I want." His lips touching mine was the last sensation I felt before the darkness carried me off to dream of more exciting things.

CHAPTER 5

Kerstrande

MY HIGH hopes for the evening spiraled south quickly enough, and not in the direction I wanted them to. Being a vampire had always been good for my libido. My need for blood often ran off on others as an enhanced sex drive to release inhibitions. Forever seventeen with that sort of power—yeah, I'd abused it at first. Now when I wanted it to work, it was useless since it didn't work on Genesis at all. Every time we got hot and heavy, he got sleepy. I wondered if it was his abilities to see what others couldn't that protected him from my power.

But waste not, want not. I'd been craving him for days. I fed, only taking a little blood. He slept, curled around me like he really wanted me to stay. When I gave in and laid my head on the pillow beside his, I actually fell asleep.

The graveyards weren't new. I'd dreamt of them for years since becoming the undead. Usually my victims would pour out of their graves, reaching for me and screaming dreadful sounds that would haunt my memories for days. I never did sleep much.

This time the dream wasn't frightening but peaceful. I sat in the middle of the graveyard, seeing grass, trees, and flowers bloom in bright color around the area filled with death. So much life spilling forward. I almost felt like the sun had started shining on me again. How long had it been?

When I opened my eyes, it was almost dawn. The kid still snoozed beside me without a care in the world. Were the dreams his doing? I touched his hair, enjoying the silky smooth feel of it between my fingers. We couldn't do this. He'd be another headstone to weigh me down.

The last thing I needed was those pretty, flower-colored eyes haunting me from beyond the grave. I'd promised Anya that I would never steal another life. If only I'd been wise enough to make that promise before meeting her.

Genesis

MY CAT mewed me out of a dream that featured Kerstrande and I having a picnic on a beach that sat just feet from the graveyard. Always with the headstones. At least there were flowers there today.

The paws in my hair became a wave that surged out of the water and ripped me away from him. I came awake screaming, but Mikka only looked mildly amused. Her tail swung around in casual happiness, perched on the edge of "feed me before I bite you" rhythm.

"Holy crap, you scared me!" I told her, rubbing my eyes and trying to get the awful dream out of my head. She was worse than any alarm clock I'd ever owned and had no snooze button. I rolled out of bed feeling a little weak in the knees and made my way to the bathroom to relieve myself, then to the kitchen to fill her bowl. She munched in a purring, happy squat that made me tired just watching.

How had I gotten home anyway? Hadn't I been with Kerstrande? Or was that all a dream?

The phone rang. "Hey, Rob," I said since his name popped up on the caller-ID.

"Everything okay?"

Was that a trick question? "Yeah, I'm good. Why?" I made my way back to the bathroom, flicked the light on this time, and stared at my disastrous hair. I would so need to bleach it and redye it.

"We have practice today at the studio."

Was I off from Down Low? I glanced at the calendar on the wall in the kitchen. I didn't start until seven. "Okay. I just have to work at seven, so I'll bring extra clothes along." Brushing through my hair didn't make it look any better. How bad would I look bald?

"Are we cool?"

He'd been asking me that a lot lately. "We're cool." I was, at least. I wasn't sure if he was still having issues with me or not. Growing up together couldn't save us from all the differences we sprouted as we got older. He'd never really seemed to get over our one big variation. Mainly, me being queer.

I touched the left side of my neck while playing with my hair, and my brain registered an "Ow." *What the hell?*

"What's wrong? You got all quiet."

A bruise swelled an angry blotch of red, purple, and blue, covering the left side just above my collarbone. The same spot the spider bite had been. "I have a giant bruise on my neck."

"Like a hickey?"

I'd never had a hickey before; were they painful? "It hurts. It looks like I got hit by a baseball bat or something."

"Did you meet some pretty vampire chick who dug your neck? I hear once you show interest, they're all over you. The whole free blood thing."

Did they have to pay for blood? I tried to remember if I'd seen anything in the beverage aisle the last time I'd ventured into the grocery store. Damn. The bruise looked awful. Maybe Cris would have something to help. I'd call him right after I got rid of Rob. "No girl," I told my friend.

He sighed but then finally said, "Do you remember anything?"

Like I somehow wouldn't remember something gnawing on my neck? "Nothing that could cause the bruise I have."

"Were you drinking? You know you have no tolerance for alcohol."

"I had a chili-cheese dog in the Park." Kerstrande's lips brushing mine haunted my memory. Had it been a dream? The dreams I had of him were usually more erotic and less disappointing.

"We've got a meeting with the new manager today. If you're not well, I can stall. After all, what are best friends for?"

I gave him a weak laugh 'cause it hurt too much to do more. "I just need some sleep. Meet you at the studio later—noon-ish, okay?"

"Sure."

We hung up without saying good-bye, and I dialed Cris to ask for some alternative medicine.

"Gene." I could hear the smile in his voice. Cris was the only person I knew who loved me for all my craziness, even if he didn't *love,* love me. He knew about my second sight and spent the past few years helping me control it. We'd been off-and-on lovers for that time. I imagined his beautiful pale-green eyes, crinkled in the corners with happiness. His dark-brown hair would be spiked in nearly three inches of perfection, the very tips blond for added style. The way he said my name sounded seductive, though I knew he didn't mean to. "What are you doing up so early?"

So I filled him in on the progress of the band and all the changes that had happened in my life.

"Kerstrande Petterson, eh? He's sort of a big fish."

I sighed into the phone. "Do you believe in love at first sight?"

"Yes. Never experienced it myself but seen it in others a time or two. You think he's the one?"

Was I willing to say that out loud? No, not yet. "So the bruise...."

"Smooth subject change." He laughed. I could almost see those wide, strong shoulders of his moving. I had a major shoulder fetish. At least he made me smile even though I was exhausted. Was it okay to lust for one man but want to be with another? Cris was everyone's fantasy guy. I guess even mine. "I'll stop by the club tonight and drop something off."

"Thanks."

"Anytime, babe."

The bed called my name as I hung up for the second time. I crawled back in, Mikka curled up beside me, and I let sleep take me back into more dreams of Kerstrande.

CHAPTER 6

JOEL got me out of bed. He arrived a little before eleven with a bucket of freshly fried chicken and some excuse about how I needed more protein. The chicken would last me a couple days, and I was as thankful for the free food as I was for the wake-up call. I arrived at the studio just in time.

We performed for a man with dark hair and glasses. He had the sinister, bad-guy look most Japanese anime gave to men with glasses. When I remarked on it to Rob, he just laughed and told me not all people with vision problems were evil.

It wasn't my best performance. The producer whined about my hair, which was purple. Thankfully I'd found a box of wash-in color under the bathroom sink. The wild color made me feel more normal than I had in days. When Rob argued with them about originality to let me keep the color, I was grateful. He had bitched at me about the heavy black eyeliner before we'd even entered the building but at least supported me in public. If I could have found my colored Sharpie set, my nails would have been purple zebra stripes, but it just would have been more for them to dislike, I guessed.

Mr. Glasses handed us each a folder. "We're starting from scratch. You'll have three months to complete fifteen tracks. Ten for the CD, the rest for special releases." The guy was Aaron Tokie, our new manager. Supposedly he'd managed Triple Flight too. I already missed my old manager.

I pawed through the stack of songs, none of which I'd written, all of which were popular crap. "I didn't write any of these."

"So?"

"Evolution has always played my songs. I write the lyrics and the melody and Rob finishes the score."

"We're establishing a fan base for you. These songs were written by seasoned songwriters and customized for your group. After two or three CDs, we may be able to add a few of your own pieces."

Sounded like corporate bullshit to me. And this was why I didn't want a big label. Devon warned me about how bad they could be, encouraged us to do it on our own. Yet I let this happen despite knowing Devon's history in the industry. I sighed. Rob and Joel looked so hopeful I bit my tongue to keep from complaining further. How could this cookie-cutter pop crap be better than my stuff?

"We've hired a voice coach for you. Feel free to play with the style, and we'll work out the differences during production."

I got style choices, how generous. I must have made an unhappy noise 'cause Rob nudged me.

"The Green room is reserved for you to practice." That was all he said before he ushered us out the door. We found the Green room easy enough. It was named for the label on the door, which said GREEN but wasn't green and neither was the room. Practicing the music didn't help. It was crap—stuff I didn't want to listen to and really didn't want to sing. Some of the songs were love songs with female pronouns. Did they expect me to pretend I was straight? I took a black Sharpie and changed the wording to make it more universal.

Our only pause was for a fifteen-minute photo shoot for some teen magazine. When I reminded the guys I had to work at seven, they decided to end the day on that note. Joel bought Chinese food, and we ate it sitting on the hood of his Mustang. Rob patted me on the shoulder. "It will work out. We can make the songs our own. Play up the rock."

Yeah. I'd do it for them. Sighing heavily, I dug into the orange chicken and brown rice. Having rich friends who liked to feed me was probably the best thing about my life at the moment.

"You remember anything more about last night?" Rob asked, sweeping my hair aside to stare at the bruise.

"Yes and no."

"What's that mean?" Joel frowned at me, stole a piece of chicken, and ate it before asking, "You get drunk?"

"No. I just don't know if I dreamt it or not. Everything's kind of weird." I stuffed a wonton into my mouth and crunched into the cream cheese center, chewed and swallowed slowly. "'Sides, it's embarrassing."

Rob slid closer. "Do tell."

I growled at him, though it didn't sound scary even to me.

"Come on, kiddo. We're pals. And I bought dinner. So talk." Joel boxed me in on the other side.

The blood that heated my cheeks embarrassed me more than the fragmented memories of last night. It wasn't like I was a virgin, so why was I blushing? I'd been little more than fifteen when one of the older kids from down the street had introduced me to sex. Cris had shown me how good it could be, and for that I was grateful. "I saw Kerstrande."

Joel raised an eyebrow. "You didn't hit him with your car again, did you?"

"No. We went somewhere. I passed out."

"Why'd you pass out?"

"He kissed me." It had happened. I'd spent the entire day convincing myself of it. There was too much in my head to ignore.

"That's weirder than those Japanese comics you read. He probably just sucked on your neck, and you passed out because his vamp powers were too much for you. The old ones can make the feeding good like that," Joel said as he dug through the fortune cookies. "I read in the paper the other day that more than fifty percent of professional musicians are vampires now. The whole immortality thing, I guess."

Both Rob and I stared at him. Did he know a lot of vampires? Joel pulled something off his car windshield and glared at it. Had someone been passing out flyers? My car didn't have one, and I was parked right next to him. He crumpled up the paper in his fist.

"It was probably just a dream," Rob pointed out. "Genesis is always daydreaming about something. We know how overactive his imagination is."

It was? I kicked a rock with my shoe. "I doubt it matters anyway. Kerstrande is like a mega star. I'm not even a blip on his radar."

"I don't know about that. Looked like you were more than a blip to me. I don't know how that boy has played straight this long. He looks at you like you're a piece of candy he wants to unwrap." Joel handed me a fortune cookie. I took the paper too and threw it on the other seat to be tossed out when I went home. "'Sides, not everyone has to have big-boobed ladies like I do. And you liking the big dog just leaves more of the ladies for me."

Rob opened the door to my car for me but didn't say a word. He couldn't handle it. Never had been able to, really. My best friend, big brother of my heart, and he couldn't accept who I was. That stung, though it didn't surprise me. He'd pulled away more and more since I left home to live on my own. Maybe it was because I wasn't trying so hard to blend in anymore.

A box of orange chicken appeared in my grip when Joel shoved past Rob and pushed the food at me. "Go home, get some rest. Dream of your guitarist idol. Tomorrow we record. You need to be the amazing singer you are, no matter what crap they make you sing. Show Tokie he gave us shit and prove to him the beauty of Evolution."

"Thanks." He was right. Joel usually was. He ruffled my hair, and I closed the door. "See you guys tomorrow."

I tore open the fortune cookie to read the little paper inside. *What you seek is right in front of you.* No kidding. I pulled out of the lot and headed for work. Sometimes being busy helped clear my head.

CRIS arrived just after midnight. The many turned heads told me he was there before I saw him. He looked like a model: muscles, definition, perfect hair, and black liner around his eyes, which met mine halfway across the room and lit up with joy. I smiled back. He was one of the only people I knew whose aura's colors changed when he saw me. It was nice to know I affected someone that way. Now only if I could do that to Kerstrande, things would be grand.

Cris gathered me into a strong hug, all shoulders and long arms. God, he had a body to dream about. We stayed that way for a few moments. I breathed in the scent of him. His otherworldliness gave me a few seconds of total calm. Whether he had powers like me, or was something other than human, didn't matter. We were two sides to the same coin. Occasional lovers who cared for each other—just not enough. I wished I actually loved him.

He brushed the hair away from my neck. "Wow, good color."

I grinned. "Yeah, if only I could turn my hair those colors."

"I brought some salve." He pulled me toward the employee locker room, the only semiprivate place in the whole building. Once inside, his expression became one of great concentration. "You feeling okay?"

"Tired, but okay. Why?" What did he see that I missed?

Cris pulled a little tub of some goo with green flakes in it out of his pocket. The stuff smelled minty. He soothed it on the bruise. The spot tingled for a few minutes but wasn't unpleasant. "Promise me you'll be careful."

"I'm always careful." That pale gaze seemed to bore right into me. I looked away. Why couldn't I love him? Even as beautiful as he was, I knew he cared for me. Why couldn't there be rainbows and starlight with him? He got me, never doubted my powers, never talked down to me. I sighed.

"You never do anything halfway."

"I don't know what you mean by that."

He just gave me that million-dollar smile of his and kissed my forehead. "And that's what I love best about you."

Kerstrande

STANDING in the corner of a gay bar hidden in shadows made me feel a lot like a stalker. My sire often followed his prey this way, but I didn't want to think of Genesis as prey. I just wanted to think of him. Watching him move had made me painfully hard. He danced to the music with a grace most men would never master. He smiled at everyone, even when turning them away. And I'd watched more than a half dozen ask him to dance or for other more intimate things.

When the brunet came in, the whole room had turned to stare. It wasn't just his appearance, which was enough to make any Hollywood model feel inadequate, but his bearing screamed of confidence and pride.

When his arms wrapped around Gene like he owned the kid, I'd had to grip the wall to keep from crossing the room and tearing him apart. And then had come the text from my sire: *Park 12:30.*

I watched the skunk-head go into a backroom with Gene. My brain and body fought which way to move. Go after the kid or follow directions from my sire? Dammit!

I finally left when the brunet came out a few minutes later wishing the kid a good night. Neither looked mussed up like sex could do, not even swollen lips. But I didn't get in my car until the other one did. I'd have to talk to Gene about his clothes, or lack thereof. Though the hair and the eyes, those I liked. Something about the liner made his lashes look even bigger, and the purple shadow.... I sighed. I really needed to stop obsessing.

When I finally found my way to the Park, anger was rolling off me in waves. Why did my sire want this meeting anyway? What right did he have to demand anything from me? Just because he was my sire, maker, and tormentor? We'd gone our separate ways years back. I owed him nothing, not allegiance, not obedience; well, maybe he deserved a good kick in the head.

I ripped the cigarette from my lips and ground it into the wood of a bench, only to immediately regret it and light another. Inhale, hold, exhale, repeat. Deep breaths. The smoke did little to ease the rage of the monster inside. Nicotine had no affect anymore, but old habits die hard. Damn him for taking that from me too.

I dropped down onto the bench as a patrolman walked by tipping his hat slightly. "Evening, sir."

Keep walking.

The man's shoulders tensed, but he moved on. People were easy to control, especially when the anger was this strong.

"Takes a lot of guts to vamp a cop, pup."

I turned to scowl at my sire, Hane Lewis, former fellow bandmate and bane of my existence. The selfish prick looked younger than he had four years ago. Only full feedings did that. Stealing the lives of others. Wasn't sixteen forever young enough for him? Humans mattered little to him, though he took a great amount of pride in seducing them. Male, female, a mix of both. Only the conquest mattered to him—that and their final death. I'd witnessed enough of that to fill ten lifetimes.

"You get caught and they'll stake you, old-fashioned-like. Maybe you'd enjoy that."

A few weeks ago I would have said yes. Any end to the life he'd cursed me with would have been great. But not anymore. Not when I kept thinking of amethyst eyes and pink hair.

"Why don't you check out first, send me a postcard from hell. Let me know when the pool is ready."

My tormentor growled and stepped forward.

"Do it!" I dared him. We'd played this game for years. His threats without follow through. "Game over. I'm ready." If I was going now, it'd be in one hell of a fight. If I could, I'd take the heartless monster with me.

"Are you? I thought you wanted this." He tossed a newspaper clipping into my lap and waited. He hadn't come for old-fashioned fisticuffs after all. The article was about Genesis and Evolution joining REA and the suspicions of our relationship. Press never missed much, and they certainly hadn't missed the way that kid looked at me.

"What do you want?" I finally asked.

He grabbed the clipping and waved it. "This to go away."

"The group? Or the suspicion that I'm doing him?"

He looked thoughtful. "He is a pretty little thing. Bet he tastes good too."

"He's mine."

"He's in my territory."

So this wasn't about the press. This was about tormenting me. "I moved when you changed the lines. He and I met in my territory."

"You should have taken him with you."

I ground the cigarette into my palm. The pain helped keep the rage from completely blackening my sight. If that happened I'd die or kill a bunch of innocent folks when my sire disappeared like the smoke he seemed to be.

The faint scent in the air of incense and rain spiked my pulse and bit through the pain. No way could I lose Genesis yet. "I marked him twice. He's mine." We couldn't fight about this. I'd lose. "I'll move him now."

A bitter smile etched Hane's lips. He was really enjoying this. Shadows pooled around his eyes, making the demon rise to the surface. Crap. The kid really did see what we were. Would he stick around if he knew about the monster inside?

In a flash, a hand gripped my throat and slammed me against the pavement. He held me there with little effort. I had to remind myself I didn't need to breathe. "He's in my territory. Means he's mine now."

I managed to nod, and he let go.

"There's a good boy."

Bastard. I bit my lip to keep from snarking at him. The wind carried the aroma of incense and rain to me. I prayed for a while, waiting for him to get bored with my lack of response and go. Finally, he straightened, towering over me like the specter he was. He'd been dead a lot longer than me, probably a couple centuries. I think it was the passage of time that really made him inhuman, rather than his need for blood. He'd forgotten what it felt like to be alive, to feel. I didn't want that.

And for all he demanded, he didn't factor in the unknown of the equation. Genesis wasn't normal. My tricks didn't work on him. He saw things no one else saw. So how likely was it that anything Hane did would work on him? But then Anya had seen things too. She hadn't deserved what she got. Genesis was a good kid. He didn't need my kind of trouble. Even if I couldn't help but be drawn to him.

The clipping burst into flames and fluttered to my feet. The last bit to be consumed was Gene's bright, smiling image. The fire licked the bottom of my pants before dying under the strong night breeze. Finally Hane vanished, whistling a cheerful tune. I cursed the bastard and rose to meet my next confrontation of the evening.

The attack left me hungry and angry again, as black-edged clouds dimmed my vision. It wouldn't be hard to convince the kid he didn't want me. If I could save one at least, please God, let me save this one.

CHAPTER 7

Genesis

A THIN curl of cigarette smoke hovered over the bench I'd sat at last night. Kerstrande dangled a lit stick from his lips. His arms were spread across the back of the bench, eyes closed. He appeared relaxed, like nothing in the world could bother him, but his eyes were covered in shadows again. They writhed like a swarm of earthworms on top of his face. How did that feel to him? Was it internal? Or did he feel them at all?

"You gonna stare all night, or do you want something from me? I bet if you take a picture you can sell it to a tabloid for some gas money." His voice made me jump a half foot in the air.

I crawled onto the bench beside him, perched on the edge so as not to get too close to that mass of moving darkness. "Are you okay?"

"As okay as I ever am. Why do you care?"

"What about last night? I only remember bits and pieces of it. I want to remember more. What happened?" I was no virgin, but I didn't feel like we'd had sex. That didn't mean we didn't do something. The bruise on my neck ached now that I was close to him again. Was he biting me? What had Rob said about hickeys? Maybe I should have asked Cris.

His shoulders stiffened. "I've no idea what you're talking about."

"I kissed you, you kissed me. We went somewhere. I got fuzzy."

Kerstrande finally turned his head to face me. I sucked in a deep breath. He looked like a skeleton, worms munching away at the non-existent flesh. "You're delusional. Don't cast your sexual fantasies on me."

"What are you?" I asked him. I'd never seen anything like it before. It was terrifying and beautiful all at once. The dark spots moved, collided, creating small ripples of colorful little rainbows like those you'd see in puddles when oil had leaked from a car.

"What the hell are *you* is the better question. Looking at me like I'm some kind of freak show when you have purple hair and see pixies in the road at night."

I ran my fingers through my hair. "The photographer for *Teen Celebs* said it looked pretty cool."

"Was he blind?"

"No, he seemed to see all right."

Kerstrande groaned and slid to a slouch. "He was humoring you."

"So you don't like it?" I tried to keep the hurt out of my voice but was pretty sure he could tell.

"No. You look like a circus clown."

"What's your favorite color? I can change it."

"Don't bother." The writhing mass grew, and it almost seemed to enshroud him for a moment before flickering back to just his face.

"I can sing for you. Make the shadows go away."

"No. Stop stalking me, would you? I don't need a kid like you following me around." He got up and headed down the path. I didn't try to go after him. His words stung too much. I headed back to my car, praying for some bit of normalcy to return to my life, even if it was a repeating ghost jumping in front of a cab.

I sat there staring into the dark until the bit of pink crumpled paper on the passenger seat caught my attention. Oh yeah, the flyer from Joel's car. I straightened it and was shocked at the horrific picture of a man on fire with several long poles sticking out of him. It was from Preservation Group, an anti-vampire advertisement. The burning vampire couldn't have been executed legally, since the federal government didn't allow torture, and he'd been tortured as though the fire wasn't enough. The image made me ill. Why had they put this on Joel's car? Were they aiming for mine? Did they know what I could see?

My heart pounded in fear. I dumped the flyer in a garbage can as I drove by. Were they watching me right now? What would they do if they found me out alone like this at night? I drove home a little faster than normal.

Home was no less dark or lonely. Same as it'd been since I'd met Kerstrande. The microwave beeped, finished with my TV dinner, and then the phone rang. I pressed the talk button and yanked the hot plastic tray out onto the counter. "Hey, Rob."

"Thought I'd call to check on you."

"Yeah?"

"Devon called."

"Yeah."

"Said you haven't been returning his calls. He sounded strange."

"I've been busy." And Devon had gotten so dark, like something was eating him from the inside out. It was hard to watch, and I knew no one else could see it but me.

A few seconds of silence lingered until he said, "Did you see *him* again?"

I didn't answer. The plastic peeled easily from the tray, and I mixed the potatoes and gravy.

"Genesis, you know I'm your friend, right?"

The sigh escaped my throat before I could stop it. "I get it, okay? I just need you to get it. I like him. Like I like the color red and the taste of chili dogs. I can't help it. So maybe I'm not normal like you. I'm sorry."

"You always say you're sorry, Gene. But are you really? Think about our future. Gay singers are musical suicide. Besides, he insults you, treats you like crap. You should just let him go."

He also kissed me like we could hold each other forever, like he accepted who I was and didn't care how weird my life could be. "I can't change who I am."

"Do you have to be so open about it? Find someone not in the public eye. Keep it low." Rob sighed. "There's a press thing on Friday. There will be girls there, even models. Maybe you just haven't found the right girl yet."

He really had no idea. I wonder what he'd do if he ever met Cris, the one man I had slept with on a semiregular basis. Would Rob demand I quit the band? Would he leave? "Night, Rob."

I hung up the phone and turned off the ringer. Sometimes it was hard to be his friend. But I guess it was probably hard to be my friend too. After picking up the tray, I headed for the futon to relax in front of the TV. Maybe I'd play some games before bed. Give my head some time to clear.

Bam! Bam! The door jumped at the force. My tray landed with a splat, food-side down. "Damn."

When I opened the door I expected to find some persistent reporter, but Kerstrande stood in the hallway, looking haunted, but shadows gone. Thankfully nothing lingered but us. Not even the nosy ghost from 18B who often rambled drunkenly through the halls at night.

Kerstrande shoved his way into the room, slammed the door shut, and kissed me before I could blink. Lips, tongue, and full open-mouthed kiss that felt like he was trying to devour me. The stubble on his chin was a total turn-on. I briefly wondered how that roughness would feel elsewhere and knew there was no way he could mistake how happy I was to be pressed against him. Damn his hot and cold moods, they made me dizzy, but I'd take what I could get.

When he finally pulled away, my legs barely held me up. He dropped to his knees and hugged me around the waist. "They said it would be this way," he grumbled against my stomach.

"Who said what would be what way?" The question itself confused me.

Kerstrande leaned back and whipped the lock closed, then looked at me in a way my dream version of him never had. "You want me, right?"

Duh. "Yeah."

"So here I am. And here you are. We have this nice little—" He glared at the futon. "It'll do."

I glanced at my makeshift bed too. It turned my mind into a mushy blur of white and red thoughts. "Am I going to pass out again?"

He peeled off his shirt. He worked out, had to; Robert worked out every day and didn't look that good without his shirt. The curved outlines of Kerstrande's abs, the dark pink nipples on a near hairless chest—

Had he said something? "What?"

"I asked if you felt fuzzy."

"No." I had to drag my eyes away from him before I could get to work on cleaning up my fallen meal. It had cost four seventy-five. One of the better microwavable ones, and the last of its kind in my freezer. At least payday was coming soon.

Kerstrande gripped my shirt and pulled me away from the mess. "Forget it—do it later."

"It will smell and stain the floor. I have to clean it up." Besides, I was still hungry.

"Forget it." This time his tone was more forceful. Something trekked through my brain but passed as quickly as it came. A glance up brought his crotch to eye level. Tan dress pants, somewhat loose in the legs, and the button unfastened. My mouth watered. Would he let me trace the outline of him through those pants? Did he go commando or wear some cute briefs?

I realized after a moment I'd been fiercely rubbing an unaffected area of the tile and quickly finished wiping up the mess. I ate the chicken. It tasted fine, screw whoever made the five-second rule.

Kerstrande let me go and sat on the futon, shirtless, appealing, looking like a fantasy come to life. I threw the towel in the hamper and lingered a little too long on the chicken bone before tossing it out and washing my hands. Finally, I turned back to him, thinking I had some sort of cool resolve put in place.

He'd fallen back on the futon, arms stretched over his head, feet on the floor, knees spread, a trail of golden hairs leading down into the half-loosened zipper. Water…. I fumbled for the pitcher and gulped down twelve ounces before he spoke again.

His expression relaxed and odd, he asked, "What's wrong?"

"I don't know what you mean."

With a heavy sigh he patted the tiny space between his body and the wall. "Come here, Genesis."

He said my name, not pop star or brat. Those things had almost become terms of endearment to me. Somehow I made it to the bed without falling down. He obviously hadn't expected me to obey, since he looked shocked for a few seconds before reaching to push my tight T-shirt up.

A smile cracked my face from ear to ear. "You said my name."

"Was that all it took? Saying your name?" His fingers felt warm on my chest. Much more of this and I'd bust without even getting naked.

"Say it again, and I'll do anything you want."

"Really?" He drew out the word like it made him think of something. "All right, Genesis." My name floated from his lips like a soft caress. He kissed my cheek, then my neck, and finally rested his lips against the bruise above my collarbone. "Feel nice?"

"Mmhmm."

He shoved me backward, rolled over to pin me to the bed, and held both my wrists in his grasp. Fuzziness began to fill my sight. I fought that scattering consciousness, not wanting to lose another encounter with him. If we were really going to have sex, I wanted to be awake for it.

"Stop fighting me," he told me. The shadows in his face darkened, flaring back to life. They poured over me like a suffocating fog, and I couldn't breathe. Fear forced me to freeze in place, sucking in tiny bits of air. "Now you're afraid? You pursued me until I want to strangle you, hold you down, and pound into you. Now here I am, and you don't want me." He sounded frustrated, but I couldn't see him through the charcoal mist until it began to edge away.

"I do so want you. You just got really dark, that's all. The shadows make it hard to breathe."

He stilled, eyes studying my face; the anger grew more subtly this time. I watched it build while tiny shadows curled around the edges of his skin. Small changes in light, some would say, but I knew what to look for.

"I'm sorry. I don't mean to make you angry. Maybe I can sing for you?" Maybe then the shadows would ease and he'd go back to his not-so-subtle seduction.

He laughed so hard he had to roll away from me. The fuzziness flowed away, as did the shadows in his face. The sound changed, but he had his head down. Was he crying? What happened? Was it wrong to still hope for sex when he was upset? How did I fix what I didn't know was broken?

After a few seconds, I wrapped my arms around his head, holding him tight against my chest, while he let out whatever it was that he'd held back for so long. Time passed. His sobbing ended. I ignored the tears to allow him to salvage some of his pride. Neither of us said anything. I began to doze.

Finally he whispered, "You're not normal."

"Is that a bad thing?" I asked into the earthy smell of his hair where I'd buried my face.

Silence again. Shrugging the blankets up around his shoulders, I snuggled in beside him, fitting my body to his. No reason for either of us to be lonely. He stiffened at first, then finally relaxed, laying his head next to mine on the single pillow.

"I'm sorry I can't make all your troubles go away."

His hand found my stomach, caressing in slow circles that inched lower. "Doesn't matter."

It did to me. I sucked in a deep breath. He didn't seem to want me to touch him back, his body going tense each time I did. Yet he continued to explore, fingers running over my flesh like it was the first time he'd touched another person. His hand stopped less than an inch from where I wanted it to be, resting on my upper thigh.

"Are you tired, Kerstrande?" I asked. "I can turn off the lamp so we can sleep." Or help you of out those horribly teasing pants.

"You want to sleep?" He sounded confused.

"I want to do whatever you want me to do."

"And if I want things other than sleep?"

Yes, *please*. "Anything."

The silence returned again, then he said, "Turn off the lamp, Genesis."

I reached over his head and flicked the light off, plunging my little apartment into total darkness. Kerstrande was warm and comfortable, like a huge extra-firm pillow. He wrapped his arms around me and pressed his hips to mine. "Sleep," he said. "We could both use the rest."

"Okay." And we did, though it took me longer to fall asleep than him.

CHAPTER 8

RINGING awoke me. Hadn't I turned off the phone? I grumbled when it continued into the fourth and fifth ring.

"What the hell do you want?" a deep voice swore into the phone. My mind swam up from sleepy happiness to recognize that voice—Kerstrande—and that the phone pressed to his ear was his cell phone.

"It's none of your business." A pause, then, "That's not my problem. I never asked for this." Another pause. "I tried that already." Another pause, this one longer; then a sigh. "So deal with it."

I rolled the covers back. My apartment was still pitch-black. I fumbled for the lamp. Something hung over the window. Tears washed the sleep from my eyes at the light's brightness.

The storm clouds gathered on Kerstrande's face again. "He's sleeping." He glanced at me. "No. I'm not waking him just so you can threaten him." Noise came from the other side of the line, like someone was shouting. "So lay the instrumental tracks today and do the vocals tomorrow."

Tracks? Vocals? Shit! The clock flipped to just before noon. I sat up and grabbed for the phone to beg and grovel my way back into my boss's good graces. Kerstrande pushed me flat on the bed.

"Just deal," was the last thing he said before snapping the phone shut and tossing it aside. He gave me an irritated glance. "What?"

"Was that Mr. Tokie?"

"Yes."

I leapt for my cardboard dresser, only to be yanked back into bed with Kerstrande pinning me to the mattress. Now was not a good time to play. "He'll drop our contract, and I'll be stuck a nobody living off ramen forever. My friends need me to be there. Let me up, KC."

"No."

"Please."

"Three months is not enough time to complete a debut worth anything. Triple Flight took a whole year to produce Flat Line, which spent more than a year at number one. Besides, when was the last time you got more than four hours of sleep?"

I pushed at him. "In case you haven't noticed, I can't afford to rest. When I'm not at the studio, I'm waiting tables and being groped by guys at a club to pay for this grand home of mine. But I guess not having money to eat and keep a roof over your head is something you'd never understand."

He let me go. I rolled out from under him and dug for clean clothes, then changed behind the screen. My heart pounded like some crazy hip-hop beat whenever he was around. There had to be more to my life than just Kerstrande Petterson. The sad thing was that everything else was just an obligation, not a desire. No one else treated me like I wasn't a freak, touched me like I was really a person, and didn't run away when they knew what I saw.

Kerstrande stepped around the screen to glare at me, not caring that I was struggling into a shirt and not yet wearing pants. "I see. You're worried you'll be branded gay and the label won't want you anymore? Didn't have to worry about that with Saxon holding your leash, did you? Seeing as how he's got quite the eye for men himself. But then you're always aiming for the rich and powerful ones, like the model who visited you at the club the other night."

EVOLUTION

My heart stopped for a painful second. This was the judgment I'd been receiving my whole life. It hurt so much hearing it come from him. "You know nothing. They are my friends, that's it. And as for being branded gay. I *am* gay and proud of it. It's your fucking label that's trying to shove it in the closet by bitchin' about my hair and putting female pronouns in my songs. *I'm* not the one hiding what I am."

"When you traveled with Wild Park, no one took interest in your group because they assumed you were Saxon's boy toy. You dropped him fast enough when you met me. You've chased me for weeks, not caring what you did to my reputation. The world thinks we're lovers whether we are or not. They believe you were with Saxon before me, that he was your sugar daddy. Does any of that matter to you?"

"Devon and I never—" He'd never even asked me on a date. I'd always sort of seen him as the older brother I'd never had.

"Doesn't matter, kid. The world sees what it wants to see." He picked up his shirt and put it on, leaving his back to me. "You swim in the fishbowl and they craft your life for you."

I finished dressing, wiping annoying tears from my cheeks. Maybe that's why Rob kept Devon and I apart. And now Kerstrande, who didn't like me at all, felt trapped, forced to me by the media. "I'm sorry. All I ever wanted was to sing." And maybe love a little. Why was that so much to ask? Why wasn't it okay to just be me?

He stood a few feet away, the light from the lamp shading him with a black silhouette, ominous but beautiful. He was so beautiful it made my heart hurt even more.

"You're pretty clueless. Probably the best way to become a pop star." We stood in silence, him refusing to look at me and me moving toward the door. "A crappy way to begin a relationship, though."

I slid into my shoes. "Can't have a relationship if it's only one-sided." Leaving felt like running, but I had nothing else to do but move forward as I always did. "Let yourself out, and don't worry about locking the door. I have nothing valuable to steal."

He said nothing as I left. I trudged down the stairs, feeling four hundred pounds heavier and terrified of the one thing that had never scared me before—being alone. How could I have grown accustomed to having him around so quickly? What if the studio didn't want me anymore, since I was obviously not willing to be quiet about my homosexuality? What if the guys didn't want me in the band now? What else could I do with my life? How alone would I be without the band, the music, and Kerstrande?

Arriving at the studio didn't lighten my mood. Rob didn't remark about the tear-stains on my face. Joel just gave me a hug and an ice cream sandwich. I worked hard, sang what they told me to, and pretended the world didn't exist outside the music. It worked for a while. Devon called at lunch to ask me to dinner. I wondered if it would have been a date and why I'd never seen him like that. But I did turn him down and texted Cris instead, who immediately seemed to sense a change even from a text message. I had to put him off until later, though he kept pinging my phone.

Mr. Tokie pulled me aside just before it was time to go and gave me a note. It read:

Have a nice life, pop star.

Kerstrande Petterson

The words took a few minutes to sink in. Though it was written on REA letterhead, I knew his writing. Had I really messed up or what? Maybe if I'd called him, apologized for leaving in a huff. I dunno. So this was it? The end of whatever Kerstrande and I could have built felt a lot like my heart breaking. Pain walloped my chest, and I struggled not to fall to the floor in a heap of quivering tears. Not like I hadn't seen it coming.

"You worked hard today. Exceptionally well. I suspect your distractions of late have been due to young Mr. Petterson. Now that we've remedied that situation, I expect your performance to continue to improve." Mr. Tokie adjusted his glasses again. He stared down at me with open dislike. "Go home. Get some rest. I'll pick you up at eight tomorrow morning." He motioned me to the door.

EVOLUTION

I left in somewhat of a daze, managing to find my way out of the building and to my car without tripping down the stairs or anything. My dirt-covered Honda laughed at me as I got in and headed to the other job. I worked until 1:00 a.m. on autopilot, then went to Cris's feeling like I could purge Kerstrande from my system by using my friend's generosity and kindness.

When I arrived at his loft, he opened the door wearing nothing but loose running shorts. His mussed-up wet hair meant he'd probably been working out and had just showered, knowing I was arriving soon. His smile made my heart ache and tears stung my sight.

He opened his arms. I threw myself into them and sobbed. "It's okay, Little One." His words were soft and comforting.

"I'm sorry."

"No need to be." Cris lead me to his couch, a huge suede monster with cushions soft enough to sleep on, and cradled me in his lap. "You want to talk about it?"

No, but yes. Instead I kissed him. He returned it with his usual skill. Until Kerstrande, I'd never thought anyone could kiss better than Cris, and it wasn't so much KC's skill as it was the things I felt for him.

Cris pulled away first, his expression soft and understanding, which just made me cry even harder. I buried my face against his shoulder. "I'm so sorry."

"Oh, Gene, I knew this day would come eventually." He held me so tight I wished it had been him that had captured my heart.

I rubbed his stomach. He caught my wrist before I could go lower. "Let me take care of you," I begged. Maybe it would help me forget.

He shook his head. "Let me just hold you awhile, okay? I think it's best if I just hold you."

Tears flooded my sight again, but I nodded and relaxed into his arms.

Cris said nothing when I couldn't do anything other than cry. He just held me and stroked my hair. For once his peaceful calm did nothing for me. When I finally left at four, he kissed me on the cheek and told me to come to him if I ever needed him for anything. He'd tried to convince me to stay, to sleep, but I couldn't be a burden to him.

Have a nice life, pop star.

The words stung like nothing else ever had. I parked my car on the street below my apartment and headed upstairs. The bed was made. How clean of him. Bastard. A new TV dinner, a mirror of the one I'd dropped last night, sat on the counter. No note or anything, but then he'd already given me one. A stab of pain lanced my chest again. Damn him.

I shoved the dinner into the freezer, yanked the blankets from the window, and peered into the dark. It was raining. At least I'd made it home before the downpour. The pattering made my place feel smaller, lonelier, and so unforgiving.

This was why people drank and sang about broken hearts. I dug out an old orange notebook. Pages of scribbled lyrics and simple melodies decorated the book. Still a few empty pages in the back waited for pen strokes. The melody I'd been toying with in my head finally had words. I squeezed my emotions onto the paper, like drops of blood escaping with my tears, and prayed sleep would take me before I purged too deep.

CHAPTER 9

THREE weeks passed with eighteen-hour workdays. I slept little, ate only when I had to, and sang on autopilot. When I did sleep, I had nightmares of the graveyard I'd dreamt of for years. Now it was empty, like sitting in a metal box, so lonely that I avoided sleep as much as I could.

We did tons of interviews and photo shoots for promotion. That Friday we rehearsed in REA's stage room, which was sorta like a small concert hall with a fully functioning soundstage, a bunch of seats, and really good acoustics. The day had arrived with a slew of groupie hangers-on, all girls, and no word from KC. The fact that I still thought about him constantly was probably why we'd been given the room and told to practice instead of record. Mr. Tokie wanted us to each play our parts and listen for the emotion of the song. All day I'd been listening to the others perform, trying to focus on whatever gave them passion and channel it into myself. I just felt so empty, and my voice sounded just as bad.

In the first row sat three groupies and Joel's girlfriend, Sarah. She'd been encouraging. Sweet, like a friend's girl should be. From the stage they all looked pretty starry-eyed to me, and that made my head hurt. What would it have been like to have a guy of my own out there watching and encouraging me? I sucked in a deep breath and cast off the thought. I really didn't want to disappoint more people. And the crappy way I'd been singing lately, I was sure that's what would happen, whether or not I flaunted my differences in front of the group.

We finished our last track and jumped off the stage. The girls surrounded us with cheering and high pitched words. "That was great!" a pretty blonde girl told me. She had pink streaks in her hair and a nose ring. Rob had introduced me to her earlier, but I couldn't remember her name. She clung to my arm and smelled like flowers and candy, which made me sneeze.

"Thanks. Maybe we can play again for you sometime." Two brunettes hung off Rob's arms. I wished I could be as comfortable as he was around the girls. The sparkling eyes bothered me more than their "girl parts." The girl Rob had chosen for me was nice, but I didn't need a groupie. I just wanted a friend.

"I'd love to hear you sing again. Maybe something abdullah."

"You mean a cappella? Without instruments?" I asked her. She wasn't all that bright, and sadly, though I didn't consider myself that smart, I really wanted someone I could talk to for a while about normal things, like the weather or music.

"That's it."

"Okay."

She sat down in a chair and stared up at me. Did she expect me to sing now? Nothing Evolution played was fit for a cappella. The only song that came to mind was Triple Flight's "Red Rose." It reminded me of KC again. I'd studied Michael Shuon, lead singer of TF, as he'd done it improv at three different concerts. Kerstrande stood behind him on the stage, sweating in the spotlight. The haunting wail of his guitar filled the silence when Michael stopped singing. That memory inspired me to open my mouth and sing. Only I made it mine, following that beautiful guitar like I could really hear it.

I sang it for *him*, contrasting notes, extending the range, and playing up the bass in my voice. I poured myself into the song with the same emotion I'd been driving into the pieces that were hidden in my orange notebook. My sanctuary. The pain and the rain, I gave it all to the music and let it run free. This time it was my voice that rang through the room, bouncing from wall to wall, changing the colors of the occupants to gold. My heart lightened. Just a little.

Kerstrande

FIRST my sire claims the kid, then the manager, whom I hired, demands I get lost. Not like the kid hadn't said as much himself. It was just like me to push him away. Probably safer if I left him alone. My sire hadn't approached him yet, and for that I was grateful. Tokie had always been one to warn the vampires away from his bands. It hadn't helped Triple Flight, but maybe he could keep it from happening to Evolution.

The rain plummeted to the ground in growing puddles that fueled my anger. I stomped through them like a spoilt child, searching the Park as if I'd find him simpering in the rain. No one played in weather like this. And Genesis hadn't come back around for days. I'd watched him work himself to the bone at that club, then go home so weary he could barely stand. Saw how other men wanted him, watched him, even tried to touch him. He brushed them all off, only allowing the one named Cris to get through the tight emotional walls he'd erected around himself. But even then, Gene's light had vanished, his smile didn't reach his eyes, and when he took a simple hug, he often looked on the verge of tears.

My fault. Just like always. I'd done the same thing to Anya.

Thunder shook the horizon and made my blood boil. The darkness was rising over my sight again. I needed to eat. The world would be clearer if my belly was full. The dull blaze of color from the Park reminded me of dried blood. Tonight, the early darkness had been a blessing, freeing me from the confines of my home long before dark. I'd wasted it griping about the kid. I needed to sink into something, burn off the need. Push the darkness back a little longer.

The sound of women trickled through the rain in the direction of the parking lot. Young heartbeats, and strong, like Genesis.

They hovered near my car, two blondes and a redhead. I liked the variety. My car brought giggles and pointed fingers. No, I wasn't overcompensating. The wheels were just whatever was popular. An easier way to feed. "It's fast, but the ride is smooth," I told the girls, sliding up behind them.

They grouped together nervously but were all smiles. Yeah, that would do. Three had to be enough to override the taste of him. "Want a ride somewhere?"

They exchanged a look, one stepped forward, the other two followed. Safety in numbers, they thought. So easy. I hadn't even had to press the answer into their heads. The lock clicked under my thumb, and I pulled the door open. They crammed in back. I curled into the front. The need ran off me and into them as naturally as the wind blew. I started the car and headed toward the outskirts of town— my territory. Banished to the middle of nowhere. That sire of mine found it a grand joke. Hunt in a town of thirty-five. I'd rather drive the hour into the city and stalk the Park, which was neutral ground. Thankfully, my retreat had the privacy I required.

The blackness began to pour into my vision. I'd waited too long to feed. They mentioned their names, though I couldn't remember them if I tried. If more of the hunger didn't bleed off, one of them might die. They wouldn't remember me interrupting their lives, but I probably would.

Every sound and memory faded into their heartbeats, thumping strong and fast. Soon. Oh God, please soon. Two of the girls kissed, my hunger releasing their inhibitions. If only that worked as well on Genesis.

Finally, I eased my car into a heavily wooded area. The deep forest scent sang of home, peace, and a more brutal sense of possession. My territory. I had a house over the ridge, still under construction. Not that anyone knew about it but me and my accountant. Maybe Genesis would live there someday. I really need to stop thinking about that kid.

I stepped out of the car, opened the door to the backseat, and stared at my dinner for the evening. Tonight, at least, they were mine. The darkness took the last of my sight, and I prayed once again I wouldn't kill any of them. Still, all I could think of was pink hair and amethyst eyes.

CHAPTER 10

Genesis

WHEN the song ended, the entire room sparkled gold, but no one said a word. If crickets could have serenaded me, they would have. Rob and Joel just stared. The girls, who had clung to them a few moments ago, sat at my feet, even Sarah. All looked like they'd gone into some kind of trance. My heart skipped a beat. "Red Rose" was my favorite ballad. Had I just ruined the song? I'd poured so much emotion into it I hadn't really thought about my singing.

"I know I've been a little off lately, but was it that bad?"

"Gene, if you sang like that every day, we'd be crazy famous already." Joel fumbled absently with a package of licorice. He stuffed several pieces in his mouth but still managed to say, "Amazing."

Rob, too, looked dazed. "We used to do covers all the time, but I guess I never realized how similar you and Michael Shuon sound. He's got training, but your range is better, and you've got passion and depth he can't compete with."

Joel handed me some licorice. "Maybe we can borrow the song for the new album. Like a tribute or something. Your talent is more rock style. We don't have to be all pop. We never really were pop."

EVOLUTION

The blonde girl tugged on my arm. "That was so beautiful, and you sang it just for me!" She wrapped her arms around me in a near death grip. The other girls followed like some kind of hive-mind mentality with similar comments and tugging. Rob and Joel pried them off, playing bodyguards till we made our way out to the parking lot. Sarah promised to distract the girls while I got away. I liked her already and told Joel I approved. He just slapped me on the back and pushed me toward Rob's car before commenting how he had two whole days with his girl and then disappearing back inside.

"That was a pretty successful Friday," Rob commented as he quietly steered his car toward my apartment.

"Yeah. Finished two tracks and had a great interview with that teen magazine." Though I couldn't remember the name of it. I'd have to call Uo and tell her to look for it. "Today was a good day. I'm way pumped."

"About the music."

"Well, yeah. What else am I supposed to be pumped about?"

"Renee."

I glanced at my friend. "Huh?"

"The girl with the pink streaks in her hair."

Oh. "She was nice."

Rob's sideways glance said he wasn't happy.

"What? She was. She liked my voice and told me how great I was. I felt like a star."

He sighed. "I handpicked her for you. She gushed, and you hated every second of it. You don't want to be worshiped. It's stupid. You're the front man, the vocalist, the focal point of the group, but you don't want attention."

"Everyone wants to be liked." Even me.

"You just want to sing."

"Sure. Having people listen and like it is a bonus."

"At least I get it now. You're this mega positive force, and you need a negative opposite. That's why Petterson fit for you. I need to find you an opposite."

He was also a guy. Rob would never get that. I didn't really want anyone right now. I had to be okay just being me first, but I kept my mouth shut and stared out the window.

"When you sang 'Red Rose', your voice kicked me in the ass. Never saw that coming. I sat there thinking, yeah, this is why we became Evolution. This is how amazing we can be. How'd you do it?"

No way was I going to tell him I'd been thinking about Kerstrande. "I just sang. That's all."

His fingers tapped the steering wheel to the beat on the radio. "I noticed that when the label made us change our stuff. Your songs may not be as pro, but it's more heartfelt, and you sing them better."

I considered telling him about the new song I'd been working on but thought better of it. The song was incomplete, unpolished, and extremely personal. If he saw it and stomped all over it, I'd have a breakdown. Some things I wasn't ready to share with the world yet, and other things the world didn't want me to.

The car stopped in front of my building. Rob patted me on the back. "Get some rest and call me. It'll be nice to have a weekend off."

"Thanks." I didn't mention to him that I was working double shifts at the club this weekend. Instead I just waved good-bye and waited until he turned the corner before racing up to change and then getting into my Honda to go to work.

The night at the club was much the same as it always had been. Lots of drooling men begging for attention from others who were so outside their range they were on another planet. I used my fake smile to rake in the tips, and when I headed home for the night, I felt pretty good about my living expenses for the next few days.

I pulled my Honda into the parking spot in front of my building just after 2:00 a.m. and got out. Another car pulled up, the back window rolled down. "Get in, Gene."

"Devon?" I didn't want this confrontation. I didn't want to lose another friend, but I couldn't deal with the darkness that was taking control of him. Not if he wasn't willing to fight it. And KC's comment about everyone thinking I was Devon's lover still bothered me a lot. I slid into the backseat because I couldn't think of an excuse not to that didn't sound like one.

"Drive around for awhile," Devon told his driver after I closed the door. The car moved slowly. The tinted glass made it hard to see anything outside. Why was everyone so dark lately?

"You've been avoiding me," he said.

"Sorta."

"Care to tell me why?"

Not really. I just stared out the window, a million questions running through my head I had no right to ask.

"Is it the shadows?"

Was that why he was sitting in the dark? "Can you turn on the light?"

The overhead dome clicked on, filling the small area with brightness. Devon looked terrible. He'd lost weight. His normal five o'clock shadow had seen several passes of the hour hand. His pale blue-gray eyes were etched with red lines. "Swirly" no longer defined him. Instead, the mass enshrouded him like a cloud of smoke that hovered several inches thick around his body. He didn't look human anymore—more like some sort of ghoul who'd broken free from the grave to find fresh meat.

The thought made me shiver. "What's happened to you?"

"I would ask you the same thing."

"I don't look like a skeleton with death hovering over his shoulder."

His laugh was harsh. "That's a matter of opinion. I've never seen your aura so dim."

I couldn't see my aura at all, ever; everyone else's, but not mine. "You won't talk to me then? Tell me what you're doing to yourself?"

Was it drugs? I know that happened to a lot of musicians, but I'd never seen anything to make me think Devon might be on something.

"I'll share if you do. I'm in control for now."

Whatever that meant. "Are you doing drugs?"

He laughed lightly. "No."

Fine, on with the hard questions then. "Are you interested in me, Devon?"

He tilted his head sideways and seemed to look at me differently. "Depends on your meaning."

"You know, *interested.*"

"Like you are in young Mr. Petterson? No."

Okay. So he didn't want to have sex with me and be with me until we were tottering, gray old fools. That was a plus. "What does that mean? What are we? Coworkers? Friends? Rivals? I don't get it."

Devon's hand slid over mine, and I felt the darkness pull away from his skin where we touched. "He doesn't like you. I don't know why. But he wants to taste you regardless."

"The swirly darkness? Is it a person?"

His smile was faint, chilly, like someone else looked at me. "It makes me think of bad things. Makes me want things from you, Ayumu."

Goose pimples rippled up my arms. No one knew my real name except my family. Not even Rob. "How?"

Devon touched my face, though it didn't feel like Devon anymore. "You can see things about me that others can't see. I can see things about you too."

"Like my name."

Devon's sigh was long and heavy. "You're so bright. I keep wondering if I take that light, will I finally be free of the shadow? Or will he completely devour me?" He pressed himself against the door, looking wary and like himself again.

"If I can help you, I want to. You're my friend." Devon had always been the big brother I never had. The kind that picks on you but won't let anyone else do so. He had been that way since the day we first met, and I'd been nothing but a starry-eyed kid, looking to learn about the music business.

"You don't know what you're offering."

I didn't, but that didn't matter. I would have done the same for Cris, Rob, Joel, or Kerstrande. "You're not well. Whatever is doing this to you, you need to let it go."

"If only I could." He moved across the seat to kiss my hair and whispered, "Forgive me for taking advantage." His words swallowed the world and yanked me into darkness long enough to begin to feel the groggy sense of dreaming, once again of the graveyard. This time I stared at a girl with amber-colored eyes. Something seemed off about her, but before I could place it, I woke up, still in Devon's arms. The car had stopped, overhead light out. Devon sobbed. What was it about me that drove these strong men to tears?

"It's okay, Devon," I told him.

He moved across the seat and opened the opposite door of the car in front of my apartment building. "I'm sorry, Gene. I hope someday you'll forgive me. You're like a little brother to me. I'm so sorry."

"For what?" I got out feeling more than a little wobbly. How long had I slept? At least he didn't look as dark or pale. Maybe crying helped. "You should eat something."

The smile that formed on his lips looked sad and ironic all at once. "I just did."

"Huh?"

"Get some rest. I'll call you in the morning. Maybe you can sing for me."

"Sure. You should hear the mad skills I've developed." The car drove away. I could still feel Devon looking at me until it vanished into the dark. At least the rain had slowed to a drizzle. After wiping my feet in the entryway, I made my way up to my apartment. It was late and felt later. I was so tired it hurt to think. My time with Devon had been only minutes, not hours. Funny, since I remembered dreaming.

I stepped out of my shoes and left them beside the door. When I turned toward the futon, ready to jump into bed, something moved by the window, blocking the light that came in. I swallowed a gasp. The light switch was three feet to the left. "Hello?"

A clunk followed by a shuffle of something being dragged across the floor forced me to dive for the light. Brightness flooded the room from the four corner lights hooked to the switch.

All my things were piled into boxes. Kerstrande had pulled the futon apart in ways I knew it wasn't supposed to be disassembled. Blood spattered his shirt, which was open to bare his chest. Shadows danced on his face even though the light shone brightly throughout the apartment. His pants were unfastened, and he dripped water from the top of his blond head to his very expensive shoes. What had he been doing out in the rain?

My voice sounded oddly rough when I asked, "Are you okay?" He didn't seem to hear me. Instead he threw the mattress on the floor and snapped the metal frame in half. "Kerstrande!"

Finally he turned, twisting the weight of whatever stormed inside of him my way. Fuzziness slammed into me, forcing me to my knees, gasping for breath.

"KC?" I could barely breathe. There was a buzzing in my head that grew louder, like a freight train roaring down the tracks. The room snapped in and out of focus. His arms wrapped around me, pulled me against him hard enough to hurt. "Are you okay? KC?"

"No," was all he replied. He licked the spot on my neck where the bruise had faded to an ugly yellow. "Soon." With a rough shove we were both on the mattress, him on top, me thanking all things holy for having splurged on the extra-soft padding. He probably had a good fifty pounds on me. The bulk of his weight kept me from moving as he kissed my face, neck, and shoulders then unbuttoned my shirt. His attention focused elsewhere eased the strain on my lungs.

I sucked in a few deep breaths before asking, "What's wrong with you?"

Again he ignored me, finding my collarbone again with his lips before sliding downward to engulf a nipple. I arched my back, pressing myself further into his warm mouth. Cigarettes and perfume masked the earthy scent of his hair. My body ached to continue, but my head reminded me of the pain he'd already inflicted.

I yanked at his hair, trying to dislodge him before I could succumb to sleep or him. The fuzziness faded while my anger grew. He still refused to acknowledge that I was anything other than a doll for his pleasure. And damn him to hell, there were stains on his pants, not blood, like on his shirt. At that moment I couldn't decide which was worse.

My heart throbbed in stabbing pains that should have become familiar in the past few days. Yet I lay there another minute or two, debating, stunned, and silent until the burning of my anger brought it all down. *Have a nice life, pop star.* Damn him for playing with me. And damn me for letting him. I rolled out from under him, off the mattress, and to my wobbly feet.

"Looks like you've already had an orgy tonight. You don't need me. So get the hell out of my home." My apartment was trashed. Not just the futon, but dishes glistened in pieces around boxes on the floor; my CD collection had been thrown into a box that left the disks pouring free from their protective jackets. And the microwave sat beside the door, missing the plug that usually kept it connected to the wall.

"What the hell are you doing? You've destroyed my home, you heartless bastard. That's all I had. Did your orgy go so wrong you had to come here and take it out on me?"

He rose from the bed to his full height, which was intimidating enough, but shadows made his face look surreal. Was he like Devon?

Was there another person inside controlling him, making him do these awful things? Or was he just that cruel?

"Me?" His voice came out low enough to sound gravely. "You smell like girls, and *him*, that Australian ex-lover of yours."

"Devon and I have never been lovers. Besides, you left me. Remember the note? 'Have a nice life, pop star.' Thanks for the souvenir, you jerk."

"So you'll do whatever will have you? Saxon's almost ten years older than you."

We so weren't going there. "I'm not the one with stains on my pants proclaiming I've had an orgy."

He glanced down at his clothes as though it were the first time he'd seen them today. I dug through my stuff searching for a blanket. Maybe some of it was salvageable. Uo would help me replace some of it. Maybe Cris would too. Odd how important the little things could become.

Kerstrande said nothing for so long I finally looked back at him, and he stood completely naked. I tried to keep from staring in dumb fascination, but my mouth went dry, and my body refused to move. He truly was the most beautiful man on earth, even as messed up as he was now.

His gaze wildly searched the apartment. "I need a bath. Have to get them off me."

I blinked, trying to pull my thoughts and eyes from his obvious desires to the one he'd actually asked for. "I don't have a tub, but there's a shower in there." I gestured toward the bathroom. He didn't move. "KC?"

"Stop saying my name like that."

"Do you prefer Kerstrande?"

He shivered. "Cold."

Maybe he was sick. I touched his arm, which made him jump. "Sorry, sorry. Just follow me."

Slowly I backed away, toward the bathroom. After I pulled back the shower curtain and flicked on the water, I waved him toward the hot stream. He didn't move. Just stared, eyes locked on my hair. Now what?

I reached out to touch his arm. His eyes followed my movement, but his skin felt like ice. Maybe he really was sick. After stripping off my own clothes, I dragged him under the spray with me. Not that he seemed to notice, until I shoved him under the warmth of the water. He shivered for several minutes while I lathered up a washrag and began to wipe away the stains of the evening.

He'd trashed my apartment, acted like a heartless jerk, and I should have been angry. He just looked so helpless, so lost, that I couldn't push him away. I could touch him all I wanted as I washed him but had to work hard not to linger too long in any particular spot. He didn't move, speak, or even breathe, it seemed. Just stood shivering, eyes on me the whole time.

"What happened to you? Did someone hurt you?" I stroked his face with the cloth. The blood washed away, but the shadows didn't ease. "At least tell me if you're hurt."

"Hungry. Cold."

If I turned the water any hotter, it would be scalding. Blankets I could do, and food. Or at least I'd had those things until Kerstrande had gone berserk. "I'll fix something to eat when you're clean. It'll be okay." My heart beat harder while I stared at his shadow-strewn face. Last time he'd looked at me like that, I'd passed out. I was pretty sure now it hadn't been a dream.

"Come with me—you're too big to carry, so you have to follow me," I told him, turning off the water and then drying him with a towel. I wrapped one around my waist after wiping away the water and then added one to his before leading him into the cool apartment. The air hit like a blast from the arctic. The futon mattress spread out easily enough. I dug through the boxes to find my blankets, making more of a mess, but covered him up and pulled him into the bed with me.

"I don't have any clothes big enough to fit you, and I'm really tired. We can wash them tomorrow. After we figure out what's wrong with you."

"It's you who's not normal." It was the most normal-sounding thing he'd said in the last forty minutes. But his expression changed too, becoming aware and dangerous all at once. I backed as far away as the blankets we shared would allow. He ripped my towel away and pulled me beneath him.

"This isn't a good idea. You're sick or something." Never mind how happy he was. I could feel him pressing into my thigh.

"Hungry."

"Okay, I can get food." I'd forgotten about that anyway. I tried to get up, but he yanked me back down and disappeared beneath the blanket. My world spun in rhythms I hadn't known existed when the heat of his mouth enveloped the most sensitive part of me.

"KC...." I tried calling him, but everything was lost in the warmth of his lips. I gripped the mattress, and his hair.

His eyes were closed, face relaxed but focused, lips looking so good.

"Oh God...." I tugged his hair while he pushed me to higher peaks of pleasure than I'd ever been before.

Finally, his lips moved away, tongue lapping upward until he found the still-fading bruise on my neck. It ached in memory. "Not yet," Kerstrande mumbled, mouth against my skin. His face was peaceful, almost like he was dreaming. His long lashes went on forever and ever. I wanted to kiss them, feel them flutter across my face. "Soon."

No kidding, soon. He wrapped his arms around me and pulled me against him close enough to almost be one person instead of two. My body nearly flew off the edge each time he touched me. My heart sung with happiness that he was truly here, in the moment, touching me like I wanted him to. I wanted him but didn't have the voice to give life to the words.

"Soon," he whispered.

No, it was more like now. The racing of my heart seemed to pour down my spine and spurt in liquid fire between the two of us, lasting so long it made me dizzy. His mouth was locked to my neck, attached like he never wanted to let go.

The fuzziness poured back in, stealing the air from my lungs. We'd need another shower, but I couldn't open my eyes. Sleepiness wrapped me in a tight embrace and dragged me down. "KC?" I called to him, voice sounding hollow and strained. Something was wrong. "K...."

CHAPTER 11

WHEN people talk about dreaming of drowning, it's likely they've never actually experienced the feeling of having water fill their lungs until the world turns to black blotches of nothingness around them. My last day of high school had been filled with such a moment, and even to this day, nearly a year later, I feared large bodies of water. Until that point, I'd loved swimming. It was my only physical skill and the one I thought I'd make it through high school with since gym was a required class.

The jock who held me down didn't usually get into the water. But that day, he and three of his buddies had all jumped in, pushed me around, and kept shoving me under. Every time I thought I could get a breath, back down I'd go until my lungs burned.

Their words meant little to me, as I'd heard them a million times before. Faggot, queer, cocksucker; they were never very original. Nothing about me back then said gay. At least I didn't think it did. I kept my hair dyed black, wore the appropriate baggy jeans and T-shirts, and never put on makeup or even nail polish. Sure I was small and skinny, but I could have been a goth kid, or just a nerd. Yet "fag" is what they called me. Nearly five years of the torment should have prepared me for anything, but I guess we all still hope for the best from people even after we see their worst day after day.

EVOLUTION

That day, I remembered looking up through the swirling water and seeing my best friend, Rob, standing at the edge of the pool watching. He'd come back as a TA from college and had been helping the gym teacher, Mr. Berry, with basic things like attendance. He helped a lot of the teachers, hung out with a lot of the jocks, and flirted with girls he had no right to be looking at, but apparently had no interest in helping me.

His expression was one of shock, I remembered. Maybe a little horror, even. I don't know all the details for sure because I blacked out while he seemed to stand frozen in place. When I came to, I was in the nurse's office, freezing, still in just the tiny gym-required, Speedo-like suit, and the second I woke up, a coughing fit hit me so hard I couldn't stop even after I started retching up blood with the chlorine water. They had to call an ambulance to take me to the hospital.

My mom asked what happened while I recovered in the hospital later that night. Rob told her some kids at school were messing around, and I'd just happened to get bumped by them a little too hard. Bumped. Ha. He said no one had been close enough to help, and the boys hadn't realized right away that I was drowning.

The feeling of the water rushing over my head, the pain of it filling my lungs, and the fear of knowing I was going to drown were things I'd never forget. Knowing my best friend, the guy I thought of as my big brother, had let it all happen—in fact, stood by and watched—broke my heart. To this day I still couldn't help but get buried in depression whenever I thought about it. And obviously it still gave me nightmares.

As the dream shifted with my memories, I thought about sitting in the principal's office a week later, him telling me the accident was all my fault, and perhaps I should look into attending another high school since delinquents like me were not welcome at Jerome High School. I'd never been in trouble the entire time I'd gone to the school. Sure, my grades were average at best, but I showed up every day, kept my head down. But he wasn't referring to actual problems

I'd caused; he was referring to my sexuality, which he'd apparently made judgments about.

I'd been sixteen, and all I could think of at that moment, as I walked out of the school for the last time, was that I was never going back. They weren't going to make me live in fear anymore, and I was going to stop hiding who I was since everyone hated me anyway. The conversation with my mom had been one of the hardest.

"Mom, I'm not going back," I told her that day.

"You want to change schools?" she'd asked. I hadn't told her the truth of what happened, but I suspected she knew. She ruffled my hair and smiled at me like I was used to. Mom was good like that. Kind and always working hard to take care of me and Uo.

I shook my head. "Mom, I'm gay." I felt the words come out and almost expected a slap or something, though my mom had never raised her voice, and certainly not her hand, to me.

"And because you're gay you can't finish school?" Sometimes she saw right through me.

"No. I'm not going back at all. I'll take the GED instead, get a job. It will be okay." Anything had to be better than all the bullying, the betrayal, and the fear.

She rubbed her thumbs over my cheeks, wiping away tears I didn't realize were falling. I was giving up, and to me that was almost worse than dying. But I couldn't go back or they might just kill me. "You know you can come home whenever you need, and I will help as much as I can. That's what moms do."

I let her hug me and cried, feeling worthless and terrified, but seeing no other option. I knew she didn't understand; she wanted me to stay with her and finish school, maybe go to college. But she was dating again, and I was just the messed-up homo kid no one really wanted.

Cris helped me get a job and study for the GED, which I, thankfully, passed. He also helped me find the tiny studio I called home. All the dependency I'd cast out on others before then, I reeled in and forced myself to deal with—food or lack of it, clothes, the junker car I bought, gas. I even took to digging in the garbage to find furniture. Life was awful, but no one tried to hurt me, not physically or emotionally. No one cared anymore, and that felt really great for a while.

In those first few weeks following my departure from school, Rob and I didn't talk at all. He called a few times, but I ignored him. I was no longer living in the shadows. No one could yell at me or tease me for wearing bright colors or dying my hair orange or piercing my ears. I painted my nails, used liner and mascara every day. People I walked by on the street didn't really care. It wasn't in their nature to look outside their own world. That was what it meant to be in New York City. And for the first time in ages, I really felt I was learning to be comfortable with myself.

It wasn't until I met Joel at one of my many auditions for other bands that I found the need to call Rob and mend the bridge between us. Joel was only a year and a half older than me, and he didn't care that I was queer; he loved my voice and wanted to make music with me. We just needed a guitarist. So I buried the hatchet and pretended I hadn't seen my best friend nearly let me die that day.

Maybe I kept dreaming of that day because I hadn't got past it yet. In reality, I wouldn't be where I was now without that day. I would have stayed in school, done what was expected of me, and continued to live in fear. I loved who I was becoming, and loved to sing, so having the freedom to do both was more than a kid like me could have imagined.

The dream began again. The feeling of the water would rise up over me, blackness would come, and then it would start over, triggering memories like the daggers they could be. The final time the water rose, it wasn't Rob I saw through the dancing water distorting my sight—it was Kerstrande. Only he was reaching for me, calling my name. I reached for him, but sleep decided we couldn't be together. At least the dream of drowning stopped.

SAM KADENCE

Kerstrande

I LAY on the floor, feeling blood seep out of me as every muscle in my body ached. My sire hadn't been thrilled to find out I'd taken Gene home with me permanently. He'd snapped a half dozen bones I was too tired and hurt to try to put back in place. At least Gene was home, safe behind the threshold of my new place, even if he'd been asleep for nearly two days.

The door creaked open, and I flinched, expecting another beating. But the person who knelt down beside me began to put the bones back in place, one painful snap at a time. I clenched my teeth, doing everything I could not to scream, trying to think of better things like fresh coffee, the sound of a guitar being played by a pro, or even the pretty brightness of Genesis's eyes. In the end I couldn't hold it in. My screams bounced off the walls, but the one trying to help continued unaffected.

He lit a candle, and only then did I recognize him by the red tint of his hair. Michael. Sweet Jesus. I sucked in heavy breaths, though as a vampire I didn't really need it. The pain made me lose consciousness for a second or two. When I opened my eyes again, it was because I smelled blood. Warm, heavenly blood. I sank my teeth into only God knows who and drank deeply.

Michael whispered softly, "You'll feel better soon, I promise. Let me take care of you."

And I did, though I stopped drinking when I felt the heartbeat of the one I was feeding from falter. I tried to pull away, but Michael held me tight. He sighed heavily when I refused more.

"You're only hurting yourself, you know."

Not true. There was a horrible snap of bone, a neck breaking, and the person he'd brought me to drink from was suddenly dead.

I closed my eyes at the surge of guilt that poured a sickening sense of dread into my gut. This life was full of so much guilt and pain. Michael had been one of the worst. Changing from my best friend, the little brother I never got to have, to the monster who sat beside me, sucking away the last of the blood from our already-expired victim.

"What are you doing here, Michael?" I asked, having to force out each word.

"Hane said you needed me, so I came. I will always come for you. Even when you toss me aside for some bright-haired child. And you do realize he is just a child, don't you? Is he better than me?"

I sighed, having dealt with this so many times before. "He's older than you were when you were changed."

"And I'm forever young, beautiful, and talented. What does he have that I can't give you, Kerstrande?"

A heart. Where had that thought come from? I glared at my old bandmate and former friend. Really, he wasn't a friend anymore; the change had taken him completely. Hane was always cleaning up his messes, his kills. I closed my eyes and just wanted to go home and wrap myself around Genesis. He was so warm and alive. He never looked at others for what he could gain from them. I let out a heavy sigh. "You and I have nothing together, Michael. I've been telling you for years."

"That's not true. You love me." He leaned down to try to kiss me, but I turned away. "You always wrote songs just for me. You promised you'd only write for me."

But that Michael was dead. Had been for a long time.

"You're probably still hungry. Let me go find you something else to eat." His movement snuffed out the candle, and I prayed he would be gone long enough for me to heal so I could move on my own. I had to get home. This odd new life that was beginning for me was something to look forward to, even if it terrified me. Some demons were easier to face. I'd rather face a pink-haired one than the dark ones that covered Michael.

CHAPTER 12

Genesis

THE sun blazed an ache into my skull through a single open window. I cringed away from the brightness, buried my face in the mass of pillows, and prayed for oblivion to take me back.

The strong earthy smell of Kerstrande surrounded me. I opened my eyes to an unfamiliar room. The window cast light across the head of the bed, but in the corner of the room, near the door and sitting in shadows, was Kerstrande. An unlit cigarette dangled from his lips, and his eyes were closed. The chair leaned against the wall. He looked younger, somehow, more innocent in the natural light.

"That's a really bad habit, you know," I told him.

His eyelids cracked open. "Bringing you to my place?"

Was this his new place? "That not so much. The smoking. You could get cancer or something."

He looked skeptical. "What do you know about cancer?"

"Read about it in a comic once."

"I saw the comics at your place. They're not even in English. I expected you to be reading X-Men or Superman. Drooling over the boys in the tight Lycra costumes."

"I'm not into the whole accentuated gender-roles thing."

He sat quietly for a minute, then said, "Do you even know what that means?"

"I know more than you'd think about sexual identity and gender roles."

He chewed on the end of his cigarette but didn't respond. His lack of snarky comments was beginning to worry me.

"So this is your new place? Little cramped." I motioned to the bed, which took up ninety percent of the room. The floors were hardwood, but this place didn't seem as roomy as his last one had been.

"I realize it doesn't double as a couch, but the bed works just fine for sleeping and sex, which is all it's needed for."

My cheeks felt hot. Had we had sex? Yeah, I guess that counted as sex. "I passed out again, didn't I?"

"You didn't miss anything."

But I felt like I had. Thankfully, I wasn't tired anymore. Kerstrande tossed a cell phone on the bed. "Call your friends."

I flipped open the phone and dialed Rob first. He picked up halfway through the opening ring. "Hello?"

"Hey, Rob."

"Genesis, shit! Where are you? Are you okay? We've been crazy worried. Even your mom is out looking for you. And some guy named Cris has called a dozen times. We were about to report you missing to the cops."

Reality clobbered me like a two-ton safe. I muffled the phone with my fist. "How long have I been asleep?"

"It's Monday afternoon," Kerstrande said.

Monday. The last day I remembered was Friday. I was supposed to work at the club all weekend. I fell back onto the bed and lay staring at the ceiling.

Rob sounded frantic. "Gene?"

"Yeah?"

"Talk to me. Your boss said you didn't show for work. No one's seen you since Friday. Devon called me Sunday asking me to check on you. And your landlord said your lease had been bought out and you'd left. What's going on?"

Wow. A lot could happen in two days. "I know less than you do."

Why did weird crap always happen to me? First I hit an ex-rock star with my car, then we get offered a contract with that rock star's record label. I find out everyone thinks I'm having sex with Devon, and now I'd just slept through nearly three days after having the most incredible sex of my life with the very same ex-rock star I'd hit with my car. Not to mention that I saw ghosts and regularly dreamed of a graveyard. Could life be any more messed up?

A few more seconds passed. "That Cris guy is beeping in again. Can I forward him this number?"

"Yeah." Another pause, then the phone beeped with a call coming in. I flipped it over to Cris. "I'm okay," I told him before he could even ask.

"You sure?"

"Yeah. I'll fill you in as soon as I have all the details."

"Okay. Call me if you need me." Cris hung up, and I flipped back to Rob.

"Do you need to go to the hospital or anything?" he asked.

"I'm fine." I felt fine. Just tired—odd since I'd slept for two and a half days.

"Are you alone."

"No."

After another pause, he asked, "Petterson?" "Yes."

Rob let out a string of curses like I'd never heard before. He ranted in the background. I held the phone from my ear until he finished the worst of it.

"Aw, that's so sweet and manly of you to want to protect me," I finally said, not feeling nice at all. Someday Rob would have to get that I wasn't some little kid he needed to protect.

"Don't mock me. I'm your friend, dammit. Pretty much your only damn friend."

I bit my lip to keep from telling him what he could do with that friendship.

"It's been almost three days. Can you find out where he's taken you so I can come get you?"

Kerstrande leaned back in his chair, eyes closed. I had the feeling he heard every word, but he didn't look interested in sharing any of his thoughts with me. "Can I call you back?"

"No way! That guy is a psycho. You can't stay with him."

"It's okay. Just give me a few minutes, and I'll call you back. I promise."

"Gene—"

I hung up on him, then switched the phone off so he couldn't redial back. Rolling over, I crawled toward the edge of the bed and Kerstrande. He tilted his head to glare at me.

"So clue me in. I've never slept through two whole days in my life. What the hell happened?"

He tossed a duffle bag on the bed, then pointed to the door to the left of where he sat. "Bathroom's that way. Get dressed unless you want to spend another two days sleeping." He got up, shoved his hands in his pockets, and left the room, closing the door behind him.

What the hell?

The bathroom was more a work of art than any I'd ever seen. Massive shower, Jacuzzi tub, and marble tile. It probably cost more to rent his bathroom than my entire studio.

After ten minutes of button pushing, I figured out how to turn the water on and took another ten to shower away the lingering sleepiness. None of my questions had been answered, and now I had more.

I toweled off, standing too long with the fabric pressed to my face because it smelled like Kerstrande. I used his hairbrush and frowned in the mirror at my reflection. My last color had been a wash-out; most of them were. Rob and Joel would probably have paid to find out what my natural color was. They assumed it was black, and I bleached it, since I was half Asian, but they'd have been wrong.

The bruise on my neck had reappeared. It looked meaner this time, though it had been nearly three days since he'd given me the hickey. He had to stop doing that. Poking at it only made it ache, so I brushed my hair over the mark, threw some clothes on, sucked in a deep breath, and went to find my on-again, off-again lover.

We needed to talk, and not just about his love bites. He needed to come clean about what he was. Sure I saw dead people all the time. I knew Cris was some sort of supernatural something, without him having to tell me. And Kerstrande was the same way. Not human, though he worked really hard to hide the fact.

The living room was smaller here too. The few boxes scattered about were actually my things. I worried briefly about Mikka when I didn't see her, but she came and went as she wanted, and I had no doubt she'd show up again. I was her home, no matter where I was. Maybe Kerstrande hadn't found his yet, since his walls were bare, and the furniture seemed out of place. Like he didn't plan on staying long.

The windows were covered against the bright light of the day. Only a single lamp added a dim glow to the room. He sprawled on the couch, cup of coffee in hand, and stared into space. Was he still sick?

I sat beside him, not really sure if I should touch him or not. He tossed a piece of paper in my lap. An address. "You can go to work, but this is where you're staying now."

Didn't I get any say? "What about my studio?"

"I bought out the end of your lease. The landlord is looking for a new tenant."

"But why? You don't even like me. And there's no way I could afford even half the rent of a place like this."

He leaned over until I felt pinned against the back of the sofa by his piercing stare. "You wouldn't be here if I didn't want you. Best get ready for work. This isn't the Hotel Petterson. Just because I'm paying the rent doesn't mean you get an allowance or anything."

I blinked at him in shock for a few moments before he kissed me on the cheek, then got up to disappear into the kitchen. Had I entered the *Twilight Zone* or what? I retrieved the phone from the bedroom, since there didn't seem to be any other phones in the place and I couldn't find my cell, and dialed Rob back. He barely heard where I was before he hung up with a promise to be there in less than an hour. An hour, which meant I was somewhere outside the city. A call to the club and an angry conversation with my boss left me unemployed. *Sigh.*

I found my way to the kitchen, which was just as high-end as his last one, and watched Kerstrande lean against the counter, cigarette in one hand, coffee in the other. I pulled my hair away from the bruise and stepped in close so he couldn't miss it.

"Why'd you do this again?"

He glared at it as if it offended him. "Temporary lapse of judgment."

"Why did you trash my place?"

Kerstrande looked away.

"Do you bruise all your lovers like this? Do they pass out when you kiss them?"

"No. Just you. You're not normal."

Damn him for never answering a question straight. Damn him for acknowledging he had other lovers. Damn him for being so beautifully messed up that I just couldn't walk away. "Why can't you just say you like me? Give me something, anything, to hold on to?"

"This your natural color?" He stared at the dull honey-wheat blond of my hair, then flicked his eyes downward. "It *is* your natural color."

My world spun in hot circles of red and gold for a few moments. How had I forgotten how good his body felt against mine? The memory made my face burn.

Kerstrande shoved me against the counter, and forced my chin up until my eyes met his. They were so clear, like settled brandy in a glass decanter on some mystery movie set. "I like this color." Briefly his lips skimmed mine, but it was just in passing before he crossed the kitchen and opened the door.

Rob stood in the hall, hand raised to knock, looking shocked, then angry. He rushed to my side. "You okay?" he demanded. "Did he hurt you?" I knew he saw the bruise when his face went white and his eyes flared wide. He instantly turned to Kerstrande. "What's wrong with you?"

Kerstrande shrugged. "It's him who's not normal. Not my fault he likes it rough."

Rob's jaw dropped. I felt like my head would explode in embarrassment. "Let's go," he said, grabbing my arm to drag me to the door.

"Genesis?" Kerstrande's deep voice caressed my name. I turned back to him, willing to become his slave and never leave his side if he asked, but he dangled a key in front of me. "Don't forget your key. Be home before dark."

With a hard swallow, I nodded and swiped the key from him. Rob led me out of the condo and down all five flights of stairs to his car. "He's insane, completely and totally mad. And so are you for staying with him. What were you thinking? You couldn't have called?"

If I'd been awake I might have, but pointing that out would only make him angrier. Kerstrande and I had taken some sort of step. In which direction, I didn't know, but I liked that he expected me home and kissed me on the cheek to sooth his snarky words.

"Tokie's having a fit because you were missing, and Joel's sick—"

"Joel's sick?" He never got sick. Ate a lot, dated endless, faceless people, and drank like a fish, but was never sick.

"Tokie said it was the flu or something. We have to keep working while he's gone. Might be out all week." Rob and I got in the car. Things were really starting to unravel in my life as I realized I no longer had a paying job.

We got to the studio and no one much seemed to care that we'd arrived, even though I'd been missing for a few days. Guess we weren't doing any photo shoots today. Making our way to our private practice room, I turned a corner and someone slammed into me. My world came to a painful stop, vision shifting briefly to black then cloudy gray as it began to refocus. I blinked a few times, trying to clear the smoky, rubber duckies that were probably circling my head. Someone sat on top of me.

"He's pretty, like an angel," a voice was saying. "Can he sing for me? I heard people say he's better than me. Make him sing for me, Hane."

Multiple heads merged into one. Spiky red hair, wide green eyes, and a young, fresh face leaned over me. Why did he look so familiar?

"Michael, get off him. You'll suffocate the kid."

The weight didn't move.

"No one's better than me. I want to hear it. Sing, kid. Sing pretty. Show me why Kerstrande likes you more than me."

Michael? Red hair, green eyes? The second I put it together, I felt like I'd been hit in the gut for a second time. Michael Shuon, lead singer of Triple Flight, sat on top of me, demanding I sing.

I opened my mouth, but all that came out was a strangled sound.

"Is he choking? Should I do CPR? Hane, help!"

"If you let him up, I think he'll be just fine."

"But he hasn't sung for me yet."

"Hard to sing while lying on the floor with someone sitting on you."

"My voice coach does it to me all the time," Michael grumbled, then glared at me. "You better sing when I let you up." Finally, he moved. I lay there a bit longer, sore, shocked, and terrified all at once. Michael Shuon and Hane Lewis towered over me, both wearing concerned expressions. I shouldn't have been starstruck—I was sleeping with their guitarist—yet here was Triple Flight.

"I think you broke him," Hane commented. He looked at me curiously with chocolate-brown eyes that matched his spiky brown hair. They both appeared the same as they had in magazine shoots and album covers years ago, like they hadn't aged at all.

"Nice to meet you, guys," Rob said from somewhere to my left. "Don't mind Gene. He's a big fan." He yanked me to my feet. Michael beamed at his words, but my jaw felt bound in wire.

Hane gestured toward the hall that led to the stage room. "Shall we?"

I really, truly had to sing for them? My look must have said something to Rob, but he dragged me along, muttering, "You know you've dreamt of this."

Inside the room, Hane took his place behind the keyboard, Rob took the guitar, and Michael stepped up to the mic, motioning me forward.

"Let's do 'Red Rose'," Rob said. "You two can sing together.

Sure, sing with Michael Shuon. If my heart beat any faster it would jump free of my chest and fly across the stage, leaving a bloody, splattered mess everywhere. Hane poured into the rhythm followed by Rob, who knew the song well enough to cover for Kerstrande's absence. Michael started right on cue. I watched him turn into a total rock god before me. Not until the chorus did I realize I was singing along. I took the second stanza, making it mine, then when the chorus came back in I took the harmony, blending my deep voice to a strong bass against his tenor melody. By the time we finished, stars were glistening in Michael's eyes as he worked to keep up with me.

The music stopped, and silence reigned. Finally, Hane clapped. "Amazing work. I believe you've been outsung, Michael."

Michael didn't look angry, more entranced, like the girls had the last time I'd sung that song. "He sings pretty."

Hane grabbed Michael's arm. "That he does. Balanced against you like a real pro. Kerstrande does have an ear for talent."

Rob patted me on the back. "Gene's an amazing singer. Thanks for playing with us. Great experience. We should get back to practice now. We have to record." Hane nodded his head to us. I followed Rob back to the Green room, more than a little dizzy.

"That was cool."

"Michael was using you. You led him around like the pied piper. He kept getting mixed up by your harmony, which made him sound great when he was actually singing the melody. Bet that guy has never had to compete like that before in his life."

"'Red Rose' is his song, though. Maybe he was mad 'cause I was changing it."

"He just sang it first. Kerstrande wrote that song. He wrote everything for Triple Flight."

Kerstrande wrote articles for many magazines and newspapers now. All freelance, none about music. Joel had been making a point to cut them out for me. I suppose it wasn't a stretch that he wrote music too. Maybe that's why he hated my songs so much.

Rob folded his arms across his chest. "Let's pump some more rock into this crap they gave us. Have something good ready for when Joel gets back."

"Okay. Maybe Hane can play for us until Joel is better."

"No way. That guy gives me the creeps."

"Kerstrande gives you the creeps too," I pointed out.

Rob smacked me in the neck, right on top of the bruise.

I yowled.

"Goes to show you how good a judge of character I am."

"That hurt, you jerk."

"I hope so. What the hell is he doing? Is he a vampire? He's not registered as one. And feeding on someone without written consent is illegal. Don't let him fuck with your head." Rob began strumming his guitar.

I blinked at his words, a bunch of things all clicking together at once. Now was not the time for theories. Work now, daydream later. Sure, I could do that. I moved toward the mic.

CHAPTER 13

I STOPPED at Joel's and slid a note under the door when he didn't answer. When I'd brought up his absence to Mr. Tokie, the man had paled and put me off. But Tokie telling me flippantly not to worry made me worry all the more that something wasn't right. When Joel didn't pick up his phone any of the ten times I called, I'd really began to panic.

"He's just sick," Rob assured me. "Probably too much drinking. You know he's worse than a fish. He'll be back in a few days."

I nodded like I agreed but made the effort to stop by his place again after I left the studio. No one came to the door, and everything was eerily quiet, so maybe Joel was sleeping. Hopefully he'd feel better soon.

Rob's words stuck with me most of the day, and I thought about them the whole cab ride home. Was Kerstrande a vampire? The newspaper had some scary story every day, either about vampires killing people or people killing vampires. If I were a normal guy and a vampire, I'd probably hide what I was too.

Did the shadows make them vampires? Did that mean Devon was one too? And why had Kerstrande gone crazy on Friday? Wasn't he feeding enough? He couldn't drink from me all the time if I passed out for days. That wouldn't be good for my career—or life in general.

101

The condo was dark when I arrived. Mikka still hadn't appeared, but I did set out her food bowl and litter box. I called for Kerstrande, knowing he wasn't home. Not surprisingly, he didn't answer.

I peeled off my shoes, flicked on the living room light, sunk into the cushy sofa, and clicked on the TV. As comfy as the place felt, something was off. Hairs rose on the back of my neck, and the chill in the air was unwelcoming. Almost like someone watched me.

The phone dinged with a new text: Cris asking for the address, then another asking again if I was okay. I keyed back absently the location of the new place and that I'd been fired from Down Low. He'd helped me get that job. Maybe he could find me another. His short note back read only "Okay."

A shiver coursed through me. Maybe I could borrow a blanket from the bed. It was crazy cold in here. So far I hadn't seen any nonliving types, so maybe Kerstrande just had a window open somewhere. I paused in the doorway to the bedroom and flicked on the light, but nothing happened. The brightness from the living room reflected into the bedroom, making the spread look light blue in its place at the end of the bed. I stepped in the room to grab it.

The dark writhing shadow beside the bed made me stop midstep. Crap. That wasn't something I'd ever seen before. "Hello?" I asked, voice barely above a whisper. "KC?" No way was it him. Why did my voice shake? I saw freaky shit all the time.

A breeze poured in from the far window, which stood wide open, the curtain missing from the rod above the sill. The shadow spread across the room, hidden by part of the bed. People didn't look like that. Not even ghosts became writhing masses of dark ooze when they lingered. They had shape—sometimes a yucky one—but they still had a form. Maybe the light made it look off somehow. It could be a bird. Yeah, probably an injured bird, I tried to convince myself.

It didn't sound like a bird as I moved toward it. More like a wounded dog, breathing hard, with long nails scraping the wood floor. Oh God, what would I see?

"Hello?"

EVOLUTION

When I stepped around the bed, a dark, cold mass smashed into me, piercing my skin and drawing blood just as the world dripped to black. My head hit the floor before I even recognized the sense of falling. White pain slammed across my brow. My lungs stopped, air freezing within them. Was this what it was like to die? A sense of pain and falling into nothing? Why could I still think and feel if I were dead?

Something screamed, loud and shrill, so loud it hurt my ears. My eyes wouldn't open. I heard a terrible hiss, like an angry cat, followed by the sound of feet pattering past me to the window. A scuffle of scratching and banging. Then silence blanketed the room.

A prickly tongue licked my face. Sight came back to my eyes, everything else still hurt, yet almost felt detached. The dark mass was gone. Mikka crouched between me and the window, glancing back a few times as if to make sure whatever had been here was gone. I wanted to hug her and thank her.

Keys jingled in the door somewhere close. I knew the weight of Kerstrande's step when he slid inside the apartment, slipped off his shoes, and hung his coat. So organized. I was the chaos in his life. Unnoted music yet to be set to a page, still so insanely connected to him, I might as well have been Van Gogh sending an ear to a lover. Mad.

"Genesis?" he called. I loved how he said my name. A soft touch, good pronunciation, gentle ending. "I bought groceries. Have you eaten?" His voice came from the kitchen. He paused near the doorway to the bedroom. "Genesis?"

His jeans hugged his hips. A fitted red sweater wrapped his broad shoulders, flushing out the highlights in his hair, which fell haphazardly around his pretty eyes. He was so beautiful. Tonight he stood shadowless, normal, and so utterly perfect I felt inadequate. Maybe it was right to die here on the floor. He had to be an angel, and I, the devil sent to spin his world into destruction.

Finally, his eyes dropped downward, he frowned and moved all at once, while I tried to remember ever seeing him smile. Maybe I didn't have that kind of power over him. How awful did that make me?

He dropped to his knees beside me. "Genesis?" He paused, listening for a minute, then his eyes widened. "Shit, breathe!" He bent over me, tilted my head back and parted my lips, not for a kiss, but to force air into my aching lungs. Twice, three times, then he pressed on my chest in rapid succession. "Breathe, damn you!" He forced air back into me, and some of the pain eased, allowing me to suck in a breath.

He lifted me in his arms, encouraging me to keep breathing while he carried me to the living room and set me on the floor. Kerstrande's expression became an odd mix of colors, light, and rainbows dancing, then finally starlight when unconsciousness took me again.

The world swung me back fast. He held me close, deep voice talking to someone. No—on the phone. It was unlike him to touch me like this. Where was my snarky lover? His lips pressed to my forehead, feeling hot enough to burn. "Stay awake for me, Genesis, please. Something's wrong with you, but the ambulance is on the way."

"Hai," I mumbled absently.

His eyes became a kaleidoscope of color when I dragged my eyes open again. So pretty, like a dream of magic might be. Every time I tried to let sleep take me back, he shook me awake again. I was talking, but couldn't remember what I said.

"You're speaking in another language. I don't understand what you're saying, but stay with me until the ambulance comes, okay?"

"Gomen," I mumbled. So tired. "Sorry."

"Gomen means sorry? Okay. I've got that one. Teach me more."

The pounding of the door made him jump. He hesitated leaving me to answer. The sweetness of that moment wasn't lost on me. I just didn't have enough energy to enjoy it. Mercifully, when his arms let me go, so did the rest of the world.

CHAPTER 14

Kerstrande

THE clock over the nursing station ticked into the new day. I'd been sitting here forever. From the moment I'd found him lying on the bedroom floor, not breathing, heart not beating, everything had become a slow descent into madness.

His blond hair, so unnaturally stunning with those slanted violet eyes, haunted me with memories of running my fingers through it. He fought for his life behind some forbidden door, and all I could think about was how his hair felt. How I'd gone from simple uncomplicated guy to a crazy stalker, I didn't know, but it must be the normal path for being with him. He made me want to lock him up a cage forever, just to protect him from the world. No one had that kind of innocence anymore, except he did.

I rose from the plastic seat and stretched, muscles straining and aching despite a feeding and some healing time. The last confrontation with my sire had not been a good one. He'd beaten me senseless for taking Genesis by force. At least he'd let me go in time to get back, before Gene awoke from the unnatural sleep that had taken him.

Selfish bastards, my sire and I.

The windowed area of intensive care kept germs from visitors, and kept me out. I didn't fit the profile of family, even claiming to be his lover. All I could do was stare at him from a distance, hoping the repetitive blip-blip of the heart monitor would keep flickering in that monotonous pattern. A steady pattern was good, or so the nurse had been kind enough to point out when she passed. I'd watched that line of peaks fall flat twice. Doctors raced to revive him with machines and technology I'd never seen. The beat returned each time.

I watched them reinflate his lungs twice. His white blood cell count dropped more than two-thirds below healthy levels. Everyone from the orderlies to the doctors speculated as to what might have happened to him. His temperature had peaked at 103 degrees. Veins had burst, and one lung had nearly detached from his ribcage.

A minor concussion kept him almost completely unconscious. Yet he was healing faster than others. Body reknitting itself like the stuff of sci-fi novels. The doctors whispered things about antibodies, and cellular repair that made no sense to me. Science had never been my strong point. If his blood levels hadn't already been low they would have sent off countless samples to their labs for testing.

Genesis looked frail, pale, and nearly lifeless. Certainly not the exuberant young man I'd come to crave over the past few weeks. My heart beat in tandem to his, slowing when his did, speeding up each time the doctors restarted it.

I was too attached.

Hadn't planned it that way. In fact, nothing had gone as planned since the day I met him. He didn't forget when I told him to, didn't do what I commanded, even his wounds wouldn't heal. Not like the rest. Each time I'd taken from him, he'd slept. Over the weekend I'd hacked into his medical files to search for a history of anemia or some less common illness. Nothing.

This was all my fault.

My feeding from him did this. He would be safe without me. Not on my sire's radar. Not lying in some hospital bed fighting for life. All my fault.

EVOLUTION

This last time I couldn't remember. Not the taste, the smell, or hardly any of the evening until I held him unconscious in my arms. Vague flashes of women cycled through my head. They'd been an attempt to satiate a hunger that only craved one thing now. Clarity hadn't arrived until I had fed from him.

I truly was a monster.

The safety glass shattered, and a dull throb from my right hand snapped me out of the daze. The ICU window crumbled around my fist. Blood spurted from the broken veins, glass jutted from the flesh, mixing with the white of bared bone. This was the monster I truly was. Couldn't he see it?

People moved around me, creating voices and pulsing hearts, bodies filled with blood. I yanked myself away, running for the door. Several tried to stop me. None succeeded. After all, the monsters always got away. Heading off into the night, with only the barest of pain in my body, most of it in my chest, all I felt was guilt.

CHAPTER 15

Genesis

SOMEONE stroked the back of my hand. Then a bright light shone into one eye, blinding me and forcing tears to squeeze out. Again to the other eye. I blinked away spots until the familiar brown hair, red highlights, blue eyes, and bright smile focused above me. Rob.

A man in a white coat moved away from us toward the door. "Don't push him. He needs rest."

Rob pulled up a chair beside me and leaned on the edge of the bed. "They took out most of the IVs and stuff earlier. You've been in and out for a couple of days, and you keep asking the same questions, so I don't think you remember any of it."

I'd lost more days? Where was Kerstrande?

Rob gripped my hand, massaging my palm. "That Cris guy is down in the cafeteria. Your mom left to get some rest about an hour ago." He gave me a forced smile. "You should have said you weren't feeling well at the studio. I'd have taken you home in a flash."

My throat felt like burnt cotton. I glanced around the room. A mass of flowers bloomed from one wall some with balloons attached.

Even with all the crazy bright colors, they didn't make the room cheery.

"Mr. Tokie sent the orchids. They're in planters, so you'll have to take them home. Mr. Lewis sent the tulips, and Mr. Shuon sent the four dozen roses." Rob rolled his eyes. "A little extreme, that one. None from me. Figured I'd take you to the next Yankees game and buy you all the chili-cheese dogs and nachos you can eat. Deal?"

I nodded.

"Thirsty?"

Again a nod.

Rob poured a glass of water from a pitcher beside the bed, then held it to my lips so I could sip. Once half the glass was gone, the nasty taste in my mouth lessened a little. "Better?"

"Thanks." My voice sounded like sandpaper put to metal. Guess I wouldn't be singing again anytime soon.

"Don't look so worried. You'll be fine. The doctors say you're healing fast. If it weren't for you cracking your skull when you fell, you'd have been out of here days ago."

The fading of the day brought memories of that writhing mass beside Kerstrande's bed. Would it follow me here? What would it do to me without Mikka to protect me again? "Don't want to stay here." Shadows already began to stretch across the room.

"Okay. Let me see if I can talk them into letting you go." He disappeared through the door before I could reply.

Cris appeared before Rob returned. His relief, reflected in his aura, felt like the sun blooming over me. He looked so different without the eyeliner and big hair. More boy-next-door, but still hot. "You look like shit," he teased.

I flipped him the finger, which just made him laugh. He yanked a bag off the floor near his feet and began pulling out clothes, stuff I usually only wore when I went to my mom's or my grandfather's temple. The clothes made my mixed blood stand out, my almond-edged eyes and pale skin, but the taste of home would be welcome. A visit to the temple could help me recharge, but I wasn't sure I'd be able to make the nearly two-hour drive north.

"You need to take better care of yourself." Cris sat on the edge of the bed while I struggled out of it to pull on something that didn't bare my ass to everyone.

"Something attacked me, Cris. Something not from this world." I knew he'd understand.

He appeared to be thinking for a while but helped me tug on my clothes and button everything in place. "There's a lot of not-nice things in the world, Gene. Many are attracted to your power."

"The whole dead people thing? They can have that."

Cris stifled a laugh. "That is part of you. Would you be who you are now without that power?" He brushed the hair out of my face. I'd so need to dye it again. "That *curse*, as you put it, is what makes you care so much about everyone else. We all question what happens when we die. You actually know."

"Not really. Just the violent ones stay, and I don't know what happens when they move on."

He nodded. "But it gives us hope for something more, right? Not just one big final stop."

"I guess." I kind of hoped the whole reincarnation thing was true and if I came back I'd come back as a happy house cat.

Rob opened the door. "You're free. Just some papers to sign!"

ROB didn't bring me home to Kerstrande's place, or even to my mom's. He drove me to his small apartment in Manhattan, a one-bedroom with a real bed in the bedroom and a futon in the living room. He acted fairly cold around Cris but lightened up when my friend left. We weren't even to the door before I asked, "Where's Kerstrande?"

"You must be feeling better if you're asking about him already."

EVOLUTION

"Rob...."

"He freaked out at the hospital. Broke a window with his fist and ran out. No one's seen him since. The tabloids are having a field day that he was there at all. REA is trying to downplay it. Saying he was there representing the label."

I closed my eyes. Had he freaked because I was sick? Did he blame himself? What sense did that make? The label didn't matter at all. I almost hoped they would tell me they wanted to end my contract. At least then I could still be me and it wouldn't matter who I spent time with.

"If the doctors had been able to find puncture marks, Petterson would be up on charges as an illegal vamp. Your blood levels were so low they had to hook you up to bags of it. The really weird part is they couldn't find your blood type. So they had your mom freaked out that the second they hooked you up to a bag you'd go into cardiac arrest."

I frowned. My mom didn't need that sort of trouble. I'd have to take her off my emergency contact list. But who else would I call?

Whatever happened to me had not been Kerstrande's fault, whether he was a vampire in hiding or not. Something had attacked me in the bedroom. That odd otherworldly crap had always been my problem. Why it was getting worse lately, I didn't know. But how to explain that to anyone else?

Kerstrande's snarky behavior kept people away from him, not because he was a vampire, but because he was uncomfortable with himself. I didn't have to be a shrink to figure that out. Maybe he was a vampire. He never stood in sunlight, only drank, didn't eat. What else made a vampire? A dislike for garlic and crosses? I didn't care much for those either. How did any of that make him a bad person?

"You know I love you like a brother, right?" Rob asked.

"Yeah."

"So don't hate me when I say Petterson is bad news."

I looked away. Whatever followed him maybe, but not him.

111

"Let's get some rest." He put sheets on the futon and brought me blankets and pillows and everything. Instead of retiring to his bed, he curled beside me just talking about the old days in school and all the stupid things we did. I laughed a little and let sleep take me back to dream of more graveyards needing sunlight.

A pounding on the door startled me out of a deep sleep sometime later. Rob groaned next to me, waking slower than I. The pounding rattled the door a second time. Finally, he glanced at me, sat up, and rubbed his eyes, then looked at the clock. Quarter to four.

Again the pounding. Damn.

Rob crossed the room ready to battle demons, flung open the door, and glared at our visitor. Kerstrande stood just outside the apartment, his face a mask of rage, colors pinging in bright rainbows across his face. Shit.

He glared at me, seeming to absorb the fact that I was lying on the futon, wrapped tightly in a blanket, and Rob was clad only in boxers. It looked bad. I could feel him go cold from across the room. His shoulders tightened, the colors darkened, and he turned to leave.

"He's crazy, Gene. Just tell him it's over already."

Kerstrande scowled and disappeared down the hall. My heart flipped over in my chest, fearing he really was leaving me. I threw off the blankets and rushed after him, wheezing the whole way. "Wait, please, wait."

Rob grabbed my arm, but I shrugged him off. He didn't understand, probably never would.

"Please, KC." I stood there panting, staring at his taut back. He had paused halfway to the elevator, shoulders tense. "Please give me a minute to get my stuff. I just need to find my shoes," I begged. He glanced back, taking in that I was fully clothed except for my shoes, I think, and gave a slight nod.

I ducked back inside to find the slip-ons Cris had left me. "It will be okay, Rob."

He ranted like I'd already left. "You nearly died. That's not okay."

"That wasn't Kerstrande's fault. He got me help, saved my life. I need to go home."

"With *him*. You barely know him. How can that be home?"

Because some people were just meant to hold our hearts. I hugged him. "Night." Rob glared holes into Kerstrande the entire way to the elevator. The ride home began quietly. No radio, as usual. I dozed for a few minutes before he finally spoke.

"Why do you hide it?"

I blinked a few times trying to make sense of what "it" was. My power? My homosexuality? "Huh?"

"Your mother and grandfather were at the hospital. You spoke in another language when you were sick. Why do you hide it?"

Oh, my heritage. I sighed. "I can pass if people don't look too closely. Life is easier if I can pass. No one questions my religion, my background, or my choices if they think I'm normal white Christian American." And crazy groups like Preservation Group didn't look my way.

"Your dad's not Asian, then?"

"Nope." I knew very little about him.

"That explains a lot."

"What? My being half Japanese?"

"That and your messed-up family."

I closed my eyes and rested my head against the window. Sure, my family was messed up, just like every other family in the world. They loved me, but I'd outcast them from the rest of their family. First as a bastard child who no one really wanted, now as a gay teen obsessing over a guy who ran hot and cold. Yeah, I guess I had surpassed screwed.

Kerstrande said nothing the rest of the drive, and neither did I. When we got to his condo, I struggled toward his apartment. How a place so nice could not have an elevator made no sense. After a half flight of stairs, he turned around, picked me up, and carefully threw me over his shoulder. Thankfully he did his best to keep me from bouncing as he mounted the stairs two at a time. Inside the doorway to his place, he set me down, dropped his keys on the table, and went into the kitchen.

Everything was so dark, just like that last time. My heart pounded, making my chest ache. "Can we sleep on the couch?" Something not so nice had been in the bedroom.

"What's wrong with the bed?" He stepped into the hall, his expression an odd mix of confusion and irritation.

Be brave, Genesis, you idiot—he hasn't kicked you out yet, I reminded myself. Still…. "I just—"

Words failed me when he vanished into the darkness of the bedroom. Kerstrande? I couldn't find the voice to call him but moved toward the bedroom, trembling. That sort of terror left a stain that would be hard to ever forget. Now Kerstrande was alone with whatever it was.

My eyes searched the room for any sign of movement, but all the shadows belonged to Kerstrande. He stripped off his clothes, pretty colors back on his face, though it was more a glow now than a shadow. I should have been excited, happy he hadn't said anything about not wanting me, but I was just tired. Thankfully the feeling of being watched was gone.

Mikka brushed by my legs, stalking around the bed and back like some kind of guard. She made me feel marginally safer. Kerstrande strode to my side in two long steps, helped me out of the borrowed jacket, and peeled off the shirt and pants. There was nothing sensual about the act, even though he stood in front of me in nothing more than a pair of tight-fitting briefs.

"Get in bed. It's late, and you need sleep."

I folded my things, stuffed them away, and stood beside the bed in just my underwear, which were not the most modest kind because Cris had chosen them. Kerstrande flipped the covers up on the side nearest the window, crawled in, and then held up the opposite side for me. I snuggled in next to him, surprised by the warmth of his embrace. He didn't hesitate to wrap his arms around me and settle the long weight of himself against my side.

A thick curtain covered the window again. "Did you find anything in here after you took me to the hospital?"

"No. Why? What did you see?"

I sucked in a deep breath, turned toward him, and buried my face against his neck, not wanting to talk about it. Sleep devoured me just seconds later.

CHAPTER 16

OTHER than rising to feed Mikka, I didn't stir for more than a few minutes the whole next day and neither did Kerstrande. The alarm clock eased me awake two days later with some quiet tunes from my favorite station. Seven in the morning, KC must have set it for me. I didn't know how well I could sing, but I'd do some warm-ups and show up at the studio with my game face on.

Breakfast was fried eggs and coffee with an almond milk creamer. The creamer surprised me because I loved it, but rarely had the money for it. Kerstrande used real cream in his, which meant he'd bought it just for me. All the food seemed to be meant for me. Cupboards full of ramen and boxed food, freezer full of microwave dinners. He never touched any of it. But I didn't comment for fear it'd make him grumpy.

All the windows in the apartment huddled behind dark shades and blinds, keeping the light out. Still, something about the sun being up seemed to bother him. When he went in one of the rooms with a window, he scratched and fidgeted. So most of the time he sat in the kitchen, away from the light. Just like that morning.

Kerstrande sat in the darkest corner of the kitchen, near the fridge, chair pressed against the wall, a couple of sheets of paper in his hand. My orange notebook lay open beside the chair. Had he been looking through it? Damn. Talk about laying out a guy's soul.

"Coffee? Eggs?" I offered.

He glanced up like he hadn't seen me enter the kitchen twenty minutes ago. "Coffee, cream, no sugar today."

I poured him a cup, then set it beside him on the counter and returned to my eggs. Today would be a good day. No more sickness. I was healing. My lungs felt better. I couldn't run a marathon, but I could sing a little.

Kerstrande appeared next to me, nearly making me flip the plate. He steadied my wrist, then plopped papers on the marble island. Sheet music, handwritten.

"What's this?" I skimmed the words, which sounded familiar. The melody reminded me—I glanced toward the orange notebook.

"Music, moron. You'd think being a singer you'd have that much figured out by now." His snippy tone made me smile. At least he was back to normal.

"Midnight Rain" by Genesis Sage and Kerstrande Petterson, the title read. My rainy-night, heartbreak song. The fleshed-out guitar line would make Rob drool. It poured across the page like the rain had washed the pain from my life that night. This version was better polished. The sad wail of the guitar, the quiet plinking of the keyboard—I could almost feel the song through the page. The vocal line ripped two and a half octave ranges, making my heart pound with excitement. If I could sing this, it would be better than "Red Rose." Rob would have to help me get the pitch right, but the rest would just flow.

"How?"

I pulled the orange notebook off the floor and flipped to the most recent entry. Comments decorated the edges of the page, a word here or there crossed out and replaced, notes on the score.

"Why don't you play any of these?" he asked in between sips of his coffee.

They were too personal. One of them, about my dreams, I'd recently finished by adding a bridge about him. Showing someone this book felt like emptying out my underwear drawer for the world, hole-y briefs and all. "Midnight Rain" was about pain so deep the melody cried, its words little more than icing to flavor the song with passion. A night I'd needed to get out to continue living. "It's just stuff."

"I didn't change much. Just fleshed out the melody, extended the range to better suit your voice." He stared at me a minute or so. The numb feeling of limbo hung in the air. I wasn't sure if I should be angry or overjoyed that he took interest in my song. Laying my head against the cool stone counter helped clarify things. "Midnight Rain" was me, bared and open. If I couldn't share that with KC, who could I share it with?

His hand brushed my forehead. "Are you still sick?" His pale eyes studied me. Finally, he took his hand away and settled an irritated look in my direction. "Don't get sentimental on me. Just thought you'd wanna record one of your own damn songs. Do whatever you want with it."

I sat up and stuffed my mouth with eggs. They were cold. Better than my foot probably would have been, had I said something stupid. KC didn't much like gratitude, or any emotion really, directed his way. Just another quirk, which made me smile when I thought of some of the sweet little things he did, only then he got grumpy because I noticed he did them.

His phone beeped. "Mr. Tokie's here to pick you up."

"You know Mr. Tokie?" I rinsed off my plate, put it in the dishwasher, and then stepped into my shoes. The toes were beginning to get worn, but it was my only pair, and I'd spent days getting the art on them just right. Was there enough in my savings to buy a new pair and still pay for gas? I so needed another job.

"I recommended him. Michael Shuon wouldn't be the singer he is today without Aaron's guidance." He nursed his coffee and began flipping through my notebook again, probably looking for the next project. I wondered at that moment what made him give up his music career. "You'd better get going. You're going to be late."

I stared at him for a few more seconds, then stood up on my tiptoes to kiss him on the lips before darting out the door. "Bye, see you later!" Sometimes it was just better to leave KC and his mood alone.

ROB and I spent several hours practicing without talking or looking at each other. Without Joel to lighten the mood, the day dragged. And no one else seemed worried that Joel wasn't back yet. In fact, he hadn't returned a single call, and according to Rob, he hadn't visited me in the hospital. And Rob's gruffness just got worse each time I spoke. Finally I turned to him. "Please don't be mad at me."

He yanked his guitar strap off and banged the guitar into its stand. "You obviously don't want my advice, so let's just keep it professional." He left the room, headed for the vending machines. "Stop following me, Gene."

"Please talk to me. I'm sorry, Rob."

"You're always sorry. Do you really mean it? Do you know why you're sorry?"

"Yes. I'm sorry that what I want isn't the same as what you want."

He stared at me, a frown forming on his face. I hugged him before he could run away again. We'd always been best buddies. I'd followed him, tried to be like him. But we weren't kids anymore.

I let him go and bowed my head. "I'm sorry. We've always been together, you and me. Almost brothers, going the same way, same goals. I wanted so much to be like you." But not anymore. Rob hadn't changed—I had. I wanted to be me, more of who I was becoming than who I'd been. "I want this. It's okay if you don't agree or even understand. I just want you to be okay with me just being me."

"What exactly do you want?"

"Kerstrande." Love, really. "The music. People to like me for being me, whatever that may be." I straightened the pages of the song Kerstrande had polished for me. This too, I wanted. My music to be what I sang.

"Kerstrande comes before your career, your friends? You barely know him."

I bowed lower, from the waist, eyes closed, holding back a tide of oncoming rejection that would be a knife to my heart. "I'm sorry, Rob." How could I explain to him what I didn't understand myself?

Rob grunted and hugged me, forcing me to stand and return the hug. "You're the weirdest guy I know." Finally he let go. "I get that this is a big deal for you, but if he ever hurts you I'm going to skin him alive."

I laughed. At least his reaction was normal today. "This is important. I want to play my music. Can we practice this?" I handed him the song. "I'd like to see if we can retake control of this thing called Evolution."

His eyes grew wide when he began to read. "You wrote this? Petterson wrote this with you?"

"I started on it a while ago. He polished it, added the score."

"Petterson hasn't written a new song in years, and he just decided to rewrite one of yours? In fact, he wrote this to maximize your voice. It's in your range, not Shuon's." Rob flipped from page to page, eyes growing wider with each turn. "All right, all right. Let's work on it. Just you and me." He shook his head. "We so need Joel back on the board."

I'd already called Joel that morning but got no answer, so we'd have to get through it on our own. After an hour of practice, I'd nailed the melody and began playing with the style, even upping the range beyond what Kerstrande had written for my voice. The vocal trainer the label provided had been a big help of late. And so long as

EVOLUTION

Kerstrande didn't complain, I'd continue to sing scales when I got up in the morning until I went to bed at night.

The door to the Green room opened just before 8:00 p.m., and both Rob and I glanced up. Hane waved us to continue. Thankfully he was alone. Something about Shuon the other day gave me the creeps. When we finished the song, Hane clapped.

"Amazing. Like it was written for your voice, your personality. The writers here are good, but not that good. Where'd it come from?"

"Gene wrote it," Rob said with all the pride of a lone rooster in a barnyard of chicks.

"Kerstrande rewrote the music and changed a few words," I told Hane.

His eyes widened. "Really?" His smile was polite, but his words sounded a little bitter. "He once vowed to never write for anyone other than Michael Shuon. May I see?"

I handed him the music, somewhat apprehensive of letting it go. At least Rob had a copy too, so if Hane swiped it, I'd still have one.

"Definitely your range. You wrote the lyrics?"

"And the main melody."

"Why aren't all your songs original, then?"

My cheeks felt hot at the comment. "Mr. Tokie didn't like my stuff."

"This is better than what we had been playing. More emotion. Not so pop-ish. More angst. This hits you in the heart and drags you through the fire as it plays. That's music." Rob held his fist over his heart.

Hane set the music on the keyboard stand and flicked it on. "Let's put it together."

Rob and I shared a look, shrugged, and took our places. What could it hurt?

The song came together in my head. Keyboard poured notes like a cold, falling rain. Guitar sang a lonely tune followed only by my voice in deep baritone filled with emotion. Not even Michael Shuon walking through the door could stop me from giving all I had to the song.

The air tightened with his presence. Maybe I was still starstruck, I dunno, but he kept moving closer, until he was practically latched to my side. An unexpected bear hug stopped my singing altogether, and the instruments died behind me.

"Michael, leave him alone," Hane commanded.

Michael's expression said a lot of things I was sure not to like. He looked hungry. The only other time I'd seen that sort of perverted expression on someone's face was the time an old man had offered to pay me for sex. I'd never ridden that train again.

"He sings pretty."

"That he does. Let him go."

"Can I have him?"

"Michael...." The warning in Hane's voice was unmistakable. It came out more of an animalistic growl. Michael stroked my hair like I was some sort of pet. The darkness that covered him reminded me of what Devon had looked like the last time I'd seen him, a black-shrouded skeleton.

Rob's eyes were wide, but probably not as wide as my own. Blood rushed through me, pounding in my ears, and I began to feel like I'd hyperventilate. "Please let me go," I managed to whisper. Shadows swelled around him like noncorporal rats scurrying up his body. The cold began to seep through my clothes, leaching the strength and warmth from me. Even at his worst, Kerstrande never got this bad.

"Everything's okay," Hane soothed. Rob's expression grew calmer, but I couldn't feel anything other than panic. Michael's grip bruised my arm. His lips hovered at my throat, making me want to throw my hands up to protect it.

"He smells different," Michael mumbled, then licked me.

Yuck!

EVOLUTION

"Yeah, he smells like Kerstrande. Let him go, Michael." This time there was so much force to Hane's words my heart paused. Michael let go. I sagged into the music stand, vowing to stay the hell away from Michael Shuon.

Hane left the keyboard, grabbed Michael by the back of his shirt, and dragged him from the room, closing the door behind them. Rob stood quietly staring at his guitar, his expression peaceful.

"Rob?"

He looked up. "Huh?"

I shook my head. "Remind me to stay away from Michael Shuon."

"Michael was here?"

How could he forget? I gripped the sheet music, stolen back from the keyboard Hane had left it on. Maybe Hane had some kind of power to make people forget. Too bad it didn't work on me. "Never mind."

Was it time to go home yet? I wanted to cuddle up with KC, even if he was in a mood, just to erase the last ten minutes of my life. Thankfully, Tokie released us shortly afterward, and I made my way home.

The soft flow of an acoustic guitar playing from inside the apartment made me pause just outside the door, key in the lock. Kerstrande had never played in the short time I knew him. I had never even seen a guitar among his things. Would he stop if I entered? The melody sounded familiar. One of his old songs, maybe?

Finally, I let curiosity get the better of me and opened the door as quietly as possible. Kerstrande sat on the floor of the living room, guitar in hand, strumming. His eyes didn't open, nor did he look up, but he said, "Come here, Genesis."

When I didn't move from the doorway, he finally looked at me, raised the guitar from his lap, and gestured me to sit between him and the guitar. I sucked in a deep breath, both wanting and fearing the intimacy, while I made myself comfortable in his lap. My back pressed to his chest, butt snug against his groin. I could play casual too. No need to get all excited. Maybe.

He put the guitar back, arms around me somewhat awkwardly until we both settled into a relaxed embrace. Kerstrande positioned my fingers over the strings and pressed them into the hard metal. "That's middle C." He strummed once, then changed positions. "C chord."

"Okay."

"Sing."

"Sing what?"

"Hum for all I care. Just match the notes as I play them. Remember the feel of the strings and the sound they make."

I sang scales, following his lead. He kept his fingers pressed to mine. I messed up a few notes, but he didn't seem deterred since he continued. An ache began at the tips of my fingers, warning of oncoming blisters, and in my groin, telling me that having KC this close made me horny despite trying to pretend otherwise.

By the time he'd begun to remix the scales on the guitar, I could follow the changes of his fingers with my voice in time to sing the note. His hands moved like magic, taking me into a new tune faster than I ever thought possible. When he gave me a sheet of words to sing with him, I barely realized I was the one playing and singing until a pause in the middle of the song tripped me up.

He quieted the strings with his palm. "You smell like Michael Shuon."

What the hell? I sniffed my clothes but couldn't smell anything. "He came into the studio while we were practicing. Got a little weird. He was dark like Devon."

"Stay away from Saxon. Whatever these things are that you see, I'm sure you see them in Devon. Go with your instinct and stay away from that man." Kerstrande closed up the orange notebook, shoved it to the side, and put his guitar on the couch. One arm still wrapped around me kept me locked against him. "I heard you sang 'Red Rose'. That song wasn't meant for you."

The words stung. Did he think I fucked up his song? "I'm sorry." I tried to get up and make my way out of the room to save myself the humiliation of showing him tears, but he wouldn't let me go. "Please let me go."

"Sing 'Midnight Rain'."

"Why?" Why wouldn't he let me go so I could hide how he'd hurt me?

"You're hurt, angry. Fine. Put it into the song."

He wanted it—whatever. I relaxed into his arms, closed my eyes, and poured my frustration into the song. Didn't he get how much I wanted, *needed*, to be accepted by him? Even if it was for something as simple as a song? Tears snuck free while I sang, but I wouldn't look at him. He clung to me, face buried in my hair, arms like vises around my waist. I should have been happy to have him so close, listening to my voice, but I felt tired and heartbroken, lost.

The song faded, and he let me go, rising to disappear into the kitchen. "Eat something," he commanded.

SAM KADENCE

CHAPTER 17

Kerstrande

GENESIS slept curled up in a fetal position on his side of the bed. His chest rose and fell in peaceful monotony that should have lulled me to sleep. The deep baritone of his voice haunted me with the echo of pain even though he'd stopped singing hours ago.

I'd messed up again, hurt him without intending to. Always with him the emotions; he threw into his music, his life, what others couldn't replicate with skill. Like a child, he felt everything, saw everything, gave himself to everything without hesitation. I didn't know how he had survived so long without being tainted by the brutal real world, but it just made me want him more.

Our pre-bedtime confrontation, if it could be called that, pushed my patience near the breaking point. He stared at me with those large violet eyes, teary and wanting. I could easily have soothed away my hurtful words with soft caresses and endless kisses. But it wouldn't have stopped with sex.

Sitting close to him forced my hunger to rise. My resolve to keep him at a distance was for his safety as much as my own sanity. It'd been over a week since I fed. Damn him for giving me that kind of strength, and damn me for wanting more of it. I craved him constantly, not true hunger, but that nudging voice in the back of my head that said *Just a taste, only a little won't hurt anything.* If I were smart, I'd find food elsewhere before the desire took over.

I'd gone out in the sunlight that day, braving the irritating drumming and heat on my skin to find him shoes. Dodging the brightest of the sun's rays, I'd slogged through four stores. I hated to shop, but it'd taken that long to find a pair like the ones he wore in bright blue, and then when the sales clerk brought them out in three colors, it took nearly an hour to decide I was just going to buy them all. But when Genesis had stared at his toes that morning and picked lightly at the hole in the right shoe, frowning, it was all I could think of all day. And the rainbows—well, I had no idea how to fix that. Hopefully he could take care of that himself.

My watch ticked past 2:00 a.m. Had I been watching him so long already?

I slid the window open and peered into the darkness, breeze cooling and energizing on my face. A wash of moonlight decorated the room, making his skin look pale, perfect, and beautiful. Boys shouldn't look beautiful, but he did. The almond eyes, long black lashes, and thick lips were the stuff women dreamed of. His blond hair made him look exotic rather than Asian. He reacted violently whenever someone brought up his heritage. His flinch gave me an itch to pulverize someone since he'd obviously been hurt before.

I was far too attached.

A flutter of a bird outside the window yanked my attention away from him and slammed me into the here and now. A crow glared into the room from the ledge outside. Normally, animals avoided my kind. Even the scavengers wouldn't pick our flesh. They probably tasted the monster inside, smelled it from miles away.

The bird cawed at me. Gene twitched on the bed but didn't wake. The bird took off, wings stretching a large span as it flew toward the distant trees, where a dark figure stepped free of the shadows.

It all made sense now: the cold. Genesis's fear, and his illness. The window had been open that night. I'd simply attributed that to

Gene, but the moonlight pooling into the room highlighted the scratches on the floor. Claw marks. Probably from a bird much like the one that had just flown to its master.

The minions of demons didn't need an invite. Especially this one. I should have realized sooner what he wanted. The gentle sound of the breathing I had paced my own to reminded me of what could be stolen. Not this time, damn it.

Across the street, just at the edge of the trees, he raised a hand in salute, calling me out. It was all right. I'd wanted this since I smelled him earlier this evening. Of course if he wanted a fight, I'd be happy to oblige.

I shrugged into my duster, lit a cigarette, and headed down to meet my rival. This piper had a hell of an IOU for him too.

Genesis

THE sound of voices called me out of the blooming graveyard and back to reality. KC's warmth missing from the bed was the first thing I noticed. My eyes popped open when cold air brought goose bumps on my skin. Crap. At least these shadows were people-shaped. They all stood near the window, moonlight flowing right through them like some low-budget B movie.

I rolled to the edge of the bed and glared at the several visitors. "I don't know if you guys get it, but you're all dead. You should move on to wherever you need to go."

They all moved as one, turning their heads from staring out the window to look at me. I blinked at them, but they didn't move at all. They were obviously very dead, looking a lot like something had gnawed on them for a while. One girl moved her lips, and then a moment later I heard, "You see?"

"Yes. I think we've established that already. I see you. I'd like not to. So go away, please."

"Like me."

Did I like it? "Uh, sure. You're great. Can you go now?"

"Help you."

"With what?" Two could play this two-word game.

"*Kill him,*" they all said at once in a painfully harsh whisper that could have given nails on chalkboards a run for worst sound.

"Who? Kerstrande? No way. Touch him and I'll send you to whatever nasty ever-after has yet to take you." They moved toward me in a rush, the stuff of horror movies. I shut my eyes and waited for their contact, but it never came. They vanished. Instead, the apartment door opened and then slammed shut. At first I thought Kerstrande had heard me and gotten angry, but he didn't seem to notice I was there.

A few seconds later, he entered the bathroom and flicked on the light. The bright vanity bulbs stung my eyes, but I followed him anyway, afraid to ask where he'd gone. When I caught the door and shoved my way inside, only to see his back covered in bloody scratches; every normal, kind thought in my head vanished. I wanted to kill someone and bathe in their blood for hurting him.

"What the hell happened?"

He collapsed to his knees on the thick rug. Blood matted his tattered shirt and pants. The duster he usually wore had four long gashes that shredded it beyond repair. Blood dripped strongly enough to hit the floor with a "plink" that made it hard for me to breathe. I fell beside him, towel in hand, trying to stop the flow.

"Should I call an ambulance? There's so much blood." He hadn't looked this bad the night I hit him with my car. My heart raced while my eyes could only see the candy-apple-red of his life leaking from him.

A glance at his face stopped my fingers just a penny's width from his skin. The dark mist of shadowy things crawled around his features in that beautiful array of colored madness. He looked hollow, starved, and terrifying. Yet his eyes were locked on my shoulder, where the oversized T-shirt I wore to bed had bared my neck to him.

Those colorful critters warned me each time. I'd slept for days, got sicker and sicker. The last time we'd had sex he'd been like this, without the shadows, but distant and hungry. I'd never felt as torn as I did right then. My body reacted with desire of the memory begging for his touch, but my brain flashed in neon signs that something had gone wrong last time and was about to go wrong again. Fuzziness rolled over me like a semitruck plowing down the freeway.

He shoved me against the washbasin and kissed me hard. The metallic taste of blood flavored his lips. The warm slickness of his blood made it hard to hold onto him, but I clung for dear life. Then he yanked himself away. The growl that passed his lips, not even remotely human, sounded like, "Go to bed."

"But you're hurt."

"Do as I say for once, damn you. Be normal."

I backed away, heart thudding hard enough to hurt. Maybe I was having a heart attack instead of the constant heartbreak. Finally, I reached the doorway and had the choice of facing a room filled with ghosts or the shadows on his face. I would have given anything to stay with him.

"Close the door."

"Please talk to me, KC. Please…." I knelt there, just outside the doorway, wanting to touch him, anything but to be pushed away again.

"Close. The. Door."

I swung the door shut, feeling it slam on the weight that bound us together. The fuzziness vanished, but the need to be near him didn't. Why wouldn't he let me help? What was he afraid of? He had obviously wanted to bite me. I guess I was okay with that as long as he stayed with me, talked to me, and gave me a reason to be a part of his life.

After retrieving a blanket from the bed, I curled up on the floor beside the door and watched the room for more ghosts. He'd have to come out eventually. No reason either of us had to be alone until then.

I fell asleep waiting.

CHAPTER 18

THE doorbell rang at twenty to eight. I was gonna be late for work, but only because Mr. Tokie hadn't arrived yet. I really needed to talk to KC about having my Honda somewhere closer than the studio. It was a half hour drive just to get to the train.

When I opened the door, I expected it to be my manager, but it was Hane. "Hey, what's up?" Did he hear confusion in my voice?

His smile was strained. "Seen the paper yet? Or watched the news?"

"No. I overslept. So I haven't had time for TV, and Kerstrande doesn't get the paper." Not to mention how much blood I'd mopped up in the bathroom. The washer had already run twice. The white towels were still pink.

"You ready to go?" He remained in the doorway, darker than usual, hollow. Almost a shade of what Kerstrande looked like last night. "I have some news to deliver. Walk with me?"

"Has something happened to Rob?" I thought of Joel, who still hadn't returned my calls. "Or Joel?"

"No. This is more Triple Flight related than Evolution."

I glanced toward the bedroom where KC slept deeply, having stumbled from the bathroom just before dawn. He'd slammed the window shut and fallen into an unmovable heap on the bed. "Should I wake Kerstrande?"

"He already knows. If you're ready, I'm your ride to work."

"Okay." I scooped up my coat and the edited music for "Midnight Rain" and slid into my shoes before hurrying into the hallway.

Hane pulled his hood up, snapping on a pair of large dark sunglasses before stepping outside into the barely lit morning. "Never can be too careful. The press can surprise you anywhere."

"Right." I mimicked him by putting on my shades. "So what's up?" I crawled into his car, an Audi something, and strapped on the seat belt, a habit KC had forced on me.

Hane revved the engine and took off like a bullet down the street, up the ramp, and onto the highway. Due to the heavily tinted windows, the car interior was bathed in darkness. How did he drive this thing at night?

"There is going to be a lot of press around today."

Okay. I waited. There had to be more.

"Michael Shuon was attacked last night. The police are asking questions."

Attacked? Like mugged? Who would mug Michael Shuon? That was like robbing the Beatles. How bad was he hurt? Sure the guy scared me, but KC seemed to care a lot for him. "Is he gonna be okay?"

"He's dead, kid. Can't get more okay than that, I guess. Preservation Group is taking the credit for his death. They claim he was a vampire."

My mind spun from his sudden words. In fact, it hurt to breathe. Not my pain, but for KC. I wanted to go home. "Can you take me home, please?"

"Sorry, kid. Kerstrande needs some time to digest this. It's better if you stay away for a bit."

But he was my boyfriend. Crap, that sounded so high school. I just wanted to be sure he was okay. The wounds, the blood—had he done those things to himself when he found out? My eyes blurred, and I had to fight myself from begging Hane to take me home.

"A tribute will be held tonight in Michael's honor. Evolution will be playing."

"What?" How could they expect us to play now?

"Covers of 'Red Rose', 'Spin Crash', and 'Roller'."

"But Joel's sick." And those songs weren't written for me. Funny how KC's words came back to torment me.

Hane shrugged. "I guess if you're really against it we could cancel and disappoint all those grieving fans. Millions will be tuning in on TV worldwide to mourn."

Crap.

"I'll be backing you up on the board. Rob on guitar as always."

Something was so wrong with everything. My brain circled in dizzying thoughts. "How could something like this happen?"

"Don't know, kid. He was left in pieces."

PG, Preservation Group, the people who torched vampires and witches for fun. How had they known? Sure, Michael did some odd things and had been scary at times, but what made him a vampire? Even worse, did they suspect KC? My stomach churned. Thankfully, the studio emerged before us. We parked and Rob appeared beside the car, security towering around him. Endless flashes from cameras greeted us, but we ignored them and made our way inside.

Hane left us in the Green room. Mr. Tokie only appeared to hand us a stack of Triple Flight songs to practice. I kept checking on Kerstrande, calling every half an hour or so. He never picked up, so I left voice mails.

"I just don't think it's a good idea," Rob was telling me for the hundredth time.

"I agree."

"I mean, pulling off some sort of publicity stunt just because someone died? How low is that?"

"Low," I replied, which was likely why Hane hadn't used the publicity angle with me.

"It's like telling them to think of you as the next Michael Shuon." He paused and glanced back at me like he'd just heard me for the first time since we arrived. "Huh?"

"I agree. It's terrible. I don't wanna do it either." Any of it. Since when had wanting to sing come to this?

"Then why are we?"

'Cause we had the contract he and Joel had dreamt of. 'Cause people had a right to grieve and hear those songs one last time. 'Cause I'd do the right thing no matter how much I didn't want to. "He's gone. Forever gone. That's important to a lot more people than us."

Rob hugged me. He seemed to be trying not to cry. I hugged him back, not sure how to comfort something that I didn't understand. "I just keep thinking, what if it had been you?" His grip tightened.

"Then I'd move on to whatever the next life has for me. Hopefully a few would remember me and miss me a little, but I'd want them to be happy either way."

He finally let go, mopping at his face with his sleeve. "You say such grown-up things sometimes."

I raised a brow at him, daring him to continue that thought. He didn't.

"So you're okay with this?"

"No, but I can do it. Being okay is not necessary. I'm a professional." No matter what anyone else thought, the music came first.

Rob and I headed to the practice room. Hane met us, we practiced awhile, then we were all escorted to the arena. TV cameras and reporters lined the halls, all saying the same things, just out of sync enough to make the buzz sound like multiple stereos going at once. Thankfully security kept our area free. This would be a million times bigger than our debut at Hard Light.

Voices floated through the empty back halls from the filled seating area of the stadium. Standing room only. Jumbo cloth screens had been hung outside to cater to the thousands who didn't fit inside.

KC hadn't returned any of my calls. I just kept hearing the word "tragedy" over and over again. "Cut down so young." The whole world thought it was the greatest tragedy, those left behind to grieve him, like KC would hurt the most.

The dressing room had my name on the outside of it. The heaps of flower baskets, candies, and other random things left a hard rock in my gut. Was this stardom? How did Michael Shuon's death warrant all these good things for us? It all just felt like bad Karma piling up. I so needed to get to the temple and light some incense to cleanse all the bad away.

Hane vanished into his room for some quiet before the show. His shadows flickered around him, black and white fuzz, making it hard for me to focus on him. Did Rob sense it at all?

We lingered in the hall, too nervous to really find comfort in the elaborate rooms gifted to us. Rob kept pacing. His movement lulled me into a peaceful calm. I probably dozed off leaning against the wall until a voice called my name.

"Genesis." KC stepped out of my dressing room, a new long, black trench flowing around him. An unlit cigarette dangled from his lips. He must have snuck into my room while we were practicing and got tired of waiting for me to return. "Come here."

I turned toward him. Rob whispered, "Woof, woof," behind me, which set my ears burning.

"KC?" Was he upset? Should I hug him? Did he need to rage? He was always so cold to everyone, but I knew he hurt by the set of his shoulders. Not just the physical, but something put tension in his brow and a squint to his eyes. Would he let me help him through this?

He dragged me into the dressing room, closed the door, and kissed me so hard I could barely think. We stayed that way for a while, lips locked together, bodies so close nothing could come between us. His fingers played with my hair, and his breath tasted like mints. I didn't care that when he finally stopped kissing me, he just let his cheek rest on mine. My calm seemed to extend to him, since the last of his shadows faded as he held me. He looked normal and so beautiful, but sad.

"You loved him, didn't you?" Not as a lover, I realized, since KC never talked about him. They'd been in a band together for years. That meant something. I cared for Rob and Joel in much the same way.

"Not loved, love, present tense verb," he muttered. "Michael loved me. Wanted more than I could offer him."

"Like what we have?" I whispered quietly.

He nodded but wouldn't look at me. "When I turned him down, he did things that changed him...."

Things that made him the dark thing he'd become. I understood that without KC needing to tell me. Heartbreak could do terrible things to anyone. "It's not your fault."

His sigh was heavy.

"It's not. We all make our own choices, good or bad, and we have to keep moving forward with them." I ran my hands down his back, stroking it beneath the fabric of his new duster, finding a rhythm that seemed to give him a bit of peace.

A pounding on the door and a shouted reminder that I had to be on stage in five didn't move either of us for another minute or two. When KC pulled away, he wouldn't look at me. Instead, he headed toward the parking lot when he left the room, not toward the stage.

I had some songs to sing, but I'd follow him soon enough.

EVOLUTION

CHAPTER 19

I STEPPED into the spotlight feeling energized, confident, and calm. This was for the fans, not for me, but for the millions of flickering lights in the darkness. The teary-eyed listeners—who had no other way to express their disbelief that an era had ended—cried and cheered, wanting me to give them a bit of peace.

When I opened my mouth to sing Shuon's songs, I mirrored his style, swinging the octaves above my normal range to provide the proper eulogy in his tenor tone. Four Triple Flight songs, ending with "Red Rose" which I sang as my own, giving the emotion to the words that Michael never could have, ended our part with a reminder of love and loss. Everyone sang along to the last one.

The music died, and silence stretched throughout the arena while everyone cried. Rob and I left the stage, allowing Hane time to speak before the crowd. In the dark recesses of the halls behind the stage, men with flashlights led us to our dressing rooms.

Rob looked baffled, dazed, and tired. He stopped just before mine. "What the hell was that?"

"What?"

"You! Every note, the flow, the control, the range! You've always had a great voice, but I've never known you to use it that well."

Wow, that stung. "Thanks for being so supportive."

"I wasn't insulting you."

"Could have fooled me."

"I'm not the one acting like an asshole tonight."

How was I any different from usual? "I'm an asshole?" Really? After busting my balls to make this whole music thing work for him, I was the asshole? "You know, I'm so done with all this. The only reason I did this stupid contract was because you and Joel were begging for it. The only reason I'm here right now instead of with my grieving boyfriend is because of that damn piece of paper." I shook my head and decided I didn't want any of what this awful thing called "fame" was bringing. "I'm tired of you pushing me around, insulting me, telling me what to do, and shoving girls at me. I'm gay—get over it. And tonight I sang Michael's style, so apparently when I'm just me I'm not good enough for you. Well, fuck you."

"That's not what I meant."

"Could have fooled me." I headed for the door, hoping I could find a ride back to my car and then to find KC. Just some time in his arms could wipe away the troubles for a while. Damn, did he know he was so powerful?

"Stop running away and talk to me!" Rob demanded.

"I'm not running away. I'm being real. I wish for once you'd be real. Like the way you always promised to be there, protect me, be my friend no matter what. But you left me first. And don't think I didn't see you that day Grant Ross nearly drowned me in the pool. 'Cause I saw you there. I saw you turn your back. And I'm tired of trying to pretend that didn't affect me, that you didn't ignore me that day because I'm different. Don't tell me you didn't rejoice when I dropped out so you could stop pretending to not like the queer kid. So yeah, I really wish *you'd* just be real for once."

His shocked expression barely registered on me as I opened the outside door and flagged down a taxi to take me back to the studio. Before I realized where I was going, the Park appeared before me.

The pain of the day had stirred up a lot of memories I'd thought dead and buried. Crap. I so needed a break from life. Why hadn't I just gone home?

The answer was sitting on the bench I'd come to think of as ours. Smoke curled around KC's head from a lit cigarette, one of many, obviously, since the ground was covered in butts. I'd have to clean that up before we left. He stared at me, eyes hidden in the dark, but shadow-free. My heart pounded like a hip-hop beat while I remembered our time together in my dressing room. I think I really got it now, his comment about the songs not being written for me. They had been penned for a very different man, with a very distinct voice and personality. Shuon could never have sung "Midnight Rain." And just because I could sing his songs didn't mean I was supposed to. In a way, KC writing for him had been a never-ending apology for not being able to give him more.

I dropped to my knees at KC's feet and gripped the soft cotton fabric of his jeans as though it could keep me from falling out of myself. Did he know yet just how important he was to me? Did he get it? "KC, I—"

He put out his cigarette, flicking the butt away before wrapping his strong fingers in my hair. The other hand caressed my lips like he knew what I wanted to say. "Not yet."

He would freak, wouldn't he? That L-word did a lot of funny things to people. Not saying it wouldn't stop it from being fact, and I could wait a little longer to tell him.

"Don't sing like that again. Be you, not Michael Shuon." KC's clear amber eyes glistened down at me. He grieved, but he had me to hold him together. I gathered him into my arms. His head rested on my shoulder. I ignored the racking sobs that came from him while I stroked his back. Sometimes letting go was harder than holding on.

CHAPTER 20

ANOTHER week passed without shadows. The recording became a job: I showed up, sang my best, and returned home. Rob and I were at odds, my irritation with him still pulsing, his at me seemed to be growing. KC often spent nights at home with me watching TV, or he'd read while I jotted down a new song or drew on the new shoes he'd given me.

When he'd gifted me with three boxes, each holding a different color canvas shoe—one red, one blue, and one purple—he'd looked a lot like a little kid seeking approval. And when he'd pulled out a jumbo box of bright colored, fine-tipped Sharpies for me to color on the shoes, I gave him a bone-crushing hug he'd grumbled about for hours. Every once in a while, I'd catch him smiling just a little and looking at my feet.

He still wouldn't touch me further than a hug or a kiss. Why he was so afraid of intimacy, I didn't know, but I let him have his space and took the hesitant affection he was willing to give.

I tried Joel's phone for the fifth time with no success. Three weeks and no word. Everyone assured me he was fine, resting at home—even his girlfriend Sarah said so. We'd never been all that close. Sort of a status separation. He came from an upper-class family; I hadn't. We didn't go to dinner with our families. We didn't hang at the movies or go to sport shows. But I missed his sense of humor, kindness, and acceptance of me and all the weird things I was.

The fact that the record label didn't care really bothered me. They talked about hiring a permanent replacement for him, as though he'd died or something. And Mr. Tokie shrugged it off, saying sometimes it happened. The fame got to people and then they vanished, simply because they didn't want to deal with all the pressure. But Joel wasn't like that. No one seemed to agree with me, and it was driving me nuts. Most days I felt like I lived in some sort of alternate reality than the rest of the world.

KC listened to me vent but didn't offer a solution. Cris suggested I visit Joel, but I'd tried that several times. The whole building had gone ghost town, without the ghosts, and downright creepy. No doorman, no one in the halls, no food smells, or sounds of life in general. I wondered if I called the police, would they arrest me for the call if everyone turned out to be okay? Maybe the place just had really good insulation.

Hane practiced with us almost every day, mediating conversations. Even he had grown darker, like Devon, who I hadn't seen in weeks. Was it something about me that made my friends prone to the darkness? Rob didn't have shadows, but his aura was a wash of rejection, anger, and pain.

Today was Rob's twenty-first birthday; a day when a lot of young people drank themselves silly. Neither Joel nor I seemed to be invited to the celebration. Mad at Rob or not, I was not going to let him get hurt, even if he was going to be stupid.

Mr. Tokie ended my torture around 4:00 p.m. by handing Rob a stack of cash and wishing him a happy birthday.

A gruff "Thanks," was all Rob offered before docking his guitar and heading for the door. I raced after him, falling into step beside him, even though his body language said he didn't want me there.

"If you're going to drink, will you at least let me drive you home?"

"What do you care? I'm not 'real' to you anyway."

"Look, I'm sorry I hurt you. But I'm not sorry for what I said. I just want you to accept me for being me and stop trying to ignore me or change who I am."

He paused, sighing heavily. "You really hate this music thing, don't you?"

"I love music. I love singing."

"But you never wanted the label—"

"Hey, guys. What's up?" Sarah, Joel's girl, interrupted us. Where was Joel? Was he feeling better?

"Hey, Sarah." Rob swept her up into a hug. "I'm going to celebrate being legal. Want to come? I'll buy you a few pretty cocktails."

"Sure. You coming too, Gene?"

Did I really have a choice? "Where's Joel?" I asked her.

She wrinkled her nose at me. "Home resting."

"Will he be back soon?"

Rob glared at me as he led us to his car. I crammed myself in the backseat before he could take off without me. Sarah ignored my question. Something about her seemed off tonight. Like she was pretending too hard. Both of them ignored me during the drive.

The bar mirrored the ride. I sat in the corner, often nudged by a loud, large, drunken man who hadn't shaved in a few years. Sarah planted herself firmly in Rob's lap, swaying and moving to the beat of the music with the skill of a stripper. The two sang drinking songs, chugged beer, candy-flavored drinks, and shots, and acted like best friends. Time glazed by while I nibbled on pizza, chicken wings, and taco chips until the bartender announced closing. Finally.

I dropped a stack of dirty dishes off at the counter and turned back to find Rob all over Sarah. Not that she was protesting. Every eye in the place watched like an X-rated movie played out right in front of them. If Rob's hand pushed Sarah's shirt up any farther, she'd really be putting on a show.

"Can I have a glass of ice water, please?" I asked the bartender. He poured a glass. Seconds later I strode across the room and tossed the cold liquid into Rob's face. He came up sputtering, cursing, and swinging. I ducked, which wasn't hard since he could barely stand. He plowed into an empty table and fell awkwardly on his ass onto the floor.

"Party's over," the bartender said quietly.

"No problem. Sorry for the trouble." I handed the empty glass back, then took the stack of bills out of Rob's pocket. "For the trouble." The money Tokie had given Rob left enough for cleanup and a hefty tip. I helped Rob off the floor and had to steady him several times before we could even make our way outside. "Night, Sarah. Hope Joel feels better soon."

She flinched but turned away, settling in with the other drunks.

The fresh air in the parking lot eased some of the tension in my shoulders. Never knew a place could make me so uncomfortable until I had to spend hours there. Once Rob was strapped into the passenger seat of his car, we headed for his place.

"You're a selfish prick."

He was a mean drunk. Another reason I didn't much like bars.

"You never think about anyone, do you? Sarah was nice and warm."

"And Joel's girlfriend." Maybe that didn't matter when he was drunk. Hell, maybe it didn't matter to him at all. The silence stretched between us, widening the gap that had formed over the last few weeks.

"Now I'm not good enough to talk to? Mr. High and Mighty, Zen Buddhist bastard, and all that 'do unto others' bullshit. Asshole."

Time passed slowly, and I drove like a grandma on Sunday morning. No need to have him spewing all over me because I turned the car too fast, or I had to brake at the last moment. The insults went on and on. At least we were almost to his place.

"Genesis?"

143

"Hmm?"

"I'm gonna puke."

I swerved the car over two lanes and pulled off onto the grassy area. His door opened, and he leaned over, heaving for a good ten minutes. I stared at the stars overhead and the tree line in the distance, missing KC. Hopefully he'd gotten my message about taking care of Rob tonight. The allure of drinking never made sense to me. Swallow nasty liquid until it came back up later and left you in so much pain the next day, you wanted to die. How was that a good thing?

The door closed. "I'm okay. You can go."

We reached his apartment without another incident, and I followed him inside. He moved really slow and wobbly, weaving back and forth down the hall until he got to his door. He struggled with the key for a few seconds before opening the door and heading straight to the bathroom. The door shut, and the water turned on. He heaved a few more times—not even the noise of the shower could cover that up. I huddled on the futon, wondering if I should go or not.

I made a quick call to KC and left him another message about the night, letting him know I'd be home as soon as possible. The lap blanket Rob kept on the back of the couch became a pillow while I dozed a little, waiting for him to come out of the bathroom. The water ran for almost two hours. Each time I'd fallen asleep, I jerked awake, fearing he'd fall and hit his head or something. Several times I knocked on the door, but got no answer.

Finally the water shut off. He stepped out in just a pair of boxers, towel-drying his hair. "I feel like shit," he said.

I waited, watching him for more signs of dangerous drunkenness. He looked okay, a little more sober, at least. If I could get him in bed, he'd be safe from head injuries.

"This is where you say 'You don't look like shit, Rob. You're a babe. I'd do you.'"

My expression must have said something because he sat down next to me but slid off the futon when he missed. He landed on the floor like that was what he had intended.

144

EVOLUTION

"No? I don't do it for you? I have to be tall, scary, and mean?"

I got up and tugged him up by the armpits. He struggled to stand. "Let's get you into bed so you can sleep it off." We fumbled toward his room. He would careen away, his weight pulling me with him, and I'd have to fight to keep him upright. He finally fell in a big heap on the bed but dragged me down too. He was heavy.

"What's it like? Sex with another man?" He pressed me down onto the bed. I tried to wriggle out from beneath him, but he kept his grip tight. His lower body dug into my back. He reached around and began to unbutton my pants. "I can be what you want. I get it now."

Feeling his erection through the clothes had me panicking. "Let me go, damn it!" Still he held me down. I fought like my very life was at stake, flailing, kicking, and punching. His hands pinched, teeth bit, and body bruised mine until his hips bounced a little too hard, giving me an opening. I ripped myself away from him, nearly falling in my escape.

I struggled to pull my clothes back together and made for the door. Distance, air, I couldn't breathe. Shoes, where were my damn shoes?

"Genesis?" He was behind me. Panic made me move faster. "Genesis, are you all right?"

No. I didn't know if I'd ever be all right again.

"I'd never hurt you. You know that, right?"

Obviously, I knew nothing. "I'm going home."

"Back to him."

Yes, oh God, yes.

"He's going to hurt you. I can feel it. You like boys. I get that. I can do that. I can be what you need. You don't need him."

Yes—like the air I so desperately needed while I hobbled down the hall, shoes in hand instead of on my feet—I did.

Rob grabbed my wrist. "Don't go back to him. Please don't go." His eyes glistened with tears. I'd never seen him cry before but couldn't muster up any remorse. "Please don't be afraid of me. I'm so sorry."

"Let me go." My voice sounded detached, tired, and had the sharp edge of anger. Maybe this was why KC was angry so much. Anger made everything easier to deal with. "I'll start screaming if you don't."

Rob dropped my hand. I left, using the stairs instead of the elevator because I couldn't figure out how to get the damn thing to go down. In the parking lot I stared at his car, knowing I couldn't take it, and I had no money for a cab. A call to KC came up with another voice mail. So I called Cris, who arrived twenty minutes later.

Cris saw everything. He'd always been that way. When he tried to hug me, I pushed him away and got into his car instead. "Do you need to go to the hospital?" His voice was so soft I barely heard it as he started his car and headed toward the highway.

I shook my head, just wanting to go home. Home. What a funny word. Four letters, but such a big meaning. How quickly my place with KC had become home. Not just some place I slept, but someplace I felt safe, despite the ghosts. His arms made me feel complete. "Please just take me home."

Cris nodded, his free hand holding onto mine and massaging my palm as we drove. It was relaxing, and I napped a bit before he gently shook me awake. He offered to walk me up, but I feared falling apart if he kept treating me with kid gloves.

The condo sat dark and empty. I needed KC, his touch, his pretty eyes. Even a sneer on his snarky lips would be okay. Silence greeted me instead. Several ghosts peered at me from the bedroom, eyes wide and staring.

The memory of Rob's hands crawled across my skin. Ignoring the hangers-on, I sought the shower, turning it to hot and collapsing to the floor to let the heat burn away the unwanted touch. I'd worked at the club for more than a year, been groped a thousand times, but this was something different. Each time someone touched me at work, I made sure to stay a reasonable distance away. Friends shouldn't cross those lines. Maybe Rob and I really never had been friends. My heart ached.

A female ghost followed me into the bathroom and sat on the edge of the toilet, humming softly, comfortingly. "Poor baby. Bad night. Bad thing."

Could she hear my thoughts? How else would she know what happened? Tears streamed from my eyes. I rolled up into a ball, shaking and sobbing. He hadn't done anything other than touch me. Why was I so upset? Why couldn't I get the feeling to go away?

"Like you," the girl whispered.

"Yeah? Well, I've had enough of people liking me. So keep your hands to yourself," I snapped at her.

She smiled. "Hands off."

"Good." I wasted more than an hour beneath the scalding spray of the shower. When I returned to the room, I ripped KC's blue blanket off the bed and wrapped myself in it as though it could shield me from the worst of life. My heart pounded for a while, but the girl ghost stayed by my side, humming and soothing me until I could finally nod off. This time my dreams were sweet. No friends tried to rape me, boyfriends were always home, and ghosts weren't scary.

CHAPTER 21

THE next morning I awoke to KC puttering around somewhere outside the bedroom. The warmth and comfort of the blanket made it hard to pull myself free from bed. Finally, I got up and flicked on the lamp, realizing I hadn't put anything on last night.

I looked like I'd been raped. Teeth marks covered my back and hips. A wide array of purple and black bruises blotched my skin all over. The shower hadn't erased the hands or the damage. I ached all over.

The door opened, and KC stood in the doorway. His eyes rolled from bruise to bite and back again. His expression said rage. Shadows poured into his face. Not even the pretty ones this time. His accusatory gaze hurt something so deep inside me I didn't know what to do. I couldn't find the will to speak, barely enough to breathe, where to start? But KC had already left the room with that awful expression on his face. I pulled on some clothes and packed all I could fit of my things into a duffle bag. So much could change in just a few hours. Life could fall apart, the world could shatter, and I would be alone again.

I thought about dialing Devon for a minute or two, but didn't want to risk being stuck with his shadows too. So I sucked it up and called Cris again, who answered sleepily but promised to be on his way over. He was sort of a night owl.

"I'll be gone in a few minutes." The words hurt to say, but my own problems overwhelmed my need to sooth KC's ego today. I slipped on my shoes, made a pot of coffee, and left my key on the counter before I walked out the door. My breaking heart felt numbed, so as I thunked down the stairs, I tried to think about anything else.

Cris arrived, and I got in, only to have Mikka jump into my lap before I shut the door. Neither Cris nor I spoke during the drive. I stroked my cat and dozed a little. When we arrived in the city, I discovered he'd taken me to someplace other than his loft.

"I use this when I want some time to myself. So stay as long as you like." Cris brushed the hair out of my face. "There's a cookie jar filled with emergency cash in the back of the cupboard. You can pay me back when you hit it big. Okay?"

I nodded, feeling tears sting my sight again. If he tried to hold me, I'd completely lose control. Mikka licked my fingers and bumped my hand with her head. Cris handed me the key, his expression careful but worried. I bowed my head to him in gratitude before getting out of the car and heading upstairs.

Cris had always been such a great friend. Had I really known him only two years? Last night's events had me doubting everyone. Could I really trust him? I remembered when we met.

I HAD been club hopping, illegally. Everything was twenty-one and up and I was barely fifteen, but all my boyfriends were in their twenties. The Down Low was a great place to dance, but the guy who took me that night found another twink he liked better and ditched me. The room swayed from all the pressure of bodies and noise. So much energy. The crazy colors of other people's auras made me ill. It was awful, and the reason I never did well in school.

"He's not worth it anyway." A man sat down beside me. At first I just glanced at him, but I had to look back. He looked like a model, so beautiful, hair a pretty chocolate-brown with white streaked through the middle where his hair was spiked. His eyes were small but a pale shade of green, and his lips shaped like a long heart. "Should you be drinking?"

This beautiful man was speaking to me. "It's soda."

He smiled and it felt like the sun had broken through the building to shine just for me. "I'm Crispin, but you can call me Cris."

"Genesis," I told him.

Cris touched my hand, and the wild swirling of my senses came to a clarifying halt. "I can help you control that."

I blinked at him, fearing and hoping all at once. "Not sure what you mean." Playing dumb worked most of the time.

He leaned in close, cheek brushing mine in the most sensual way. "Your second sight, little one." My heart pulsed heavily in fear, and my chest actually hurt. His face was still pressed to mine, and he kissed my ear gently. When he pulled away, the room spun. I almost fell out of the chair. Cris wrapped his arms around me and guided me to a corner booth away from the crowd. The world righted itself again with his touch.

"Who are you?" I finally asked. The better question was what was he, but that just sounded rude to my ears.

"I already answered that, even before you asked. As to the other unanswered question, let's take some time to discover that together, okay?"

"Sure." I didn't want him to let me go again if he could keep the crazy visions from my head. "What about the dead people? Can you help me not see them?"

Cris shook his head. "I can help you control it, but they will never go away."

Any help was better than the way I had been living. "Help me, please." I remembered thinking he was so beautiful and wondering why I mattered to him at all. The years that passed afterward just brought us closer, first as lovers, then as student and teacher, then as friends. Now I wondered how I'd ever existed before knowing him. He was family to my heart. When I glanced out the window in the hall, I watched him finally pull away, still looking back, that concerned expression on his face.

This home wasn't nearly as glamorous as his other place. It felt more like a decorated apartment. Two bedrooms, an in-unit washer and dryer, and a good size kitchen, plus a big screen TV and several game consoles made it feel homey. I helped Mikka settle in, then took some cash and walked to the nearby grocery store for supplies before heading back to sulk in peace.

CHAPTER 22

Kerstrande

HE HADN'T come home. I wondered and worried where he was. This morning he'd smelled of the other man. What was his name? Robby? Bobby? Donny? The guitarist. I never missed how that man stared at Gene with a look of possession. The marks all over Genesis spoke volumes. Those sorts of bruises don't come from friendly play. Damn him for cheating on me. And damn me for caring so much.

It'd been almost a month since I fed. A month when I'd given him every last bit of myself. Rewrote his music, beat up old foes, sacrificed friends, bled for him, and starved myself. Yet the kid crawled into someone else's bed. We hadn't had sex only because it was safer for him if we didn't touch. Obviously that was all he wanted from me. I cursed myself for craving so much more than just sex and blood from him.

He'd walked out this morning so quietly, eyes heavy but downcast. Shame, perhaps? The sun set and still he didn't come back. His key had been left on the counter, like an impersonal good-bye, but I wasn't ready for that yet. I left the door unlocked, hoping he'd return and apologize or something. Wouldn't take much....

My phone rang. "What?" I demanded, not recognizing the number.

"Is Genesis all right? Is he there? He's not answering his phone." It was the guitarist.

"I'm not his keeper."

"Tell him I'm sorry. Please. Tell him I didn't mean it. I was drunk."

What the hell? Had he done something to Genesis? As I hung up, the phone beeped that I had messages. I hit one to play them back.

"Hey, KC! Just wanted to let you know that it's Rob's birthday so I'm going to make sure he gets home all right since he'll probably be drinking a lot. Miss you." Genesis's voice filled the line. The mechanical woman took over, asking if I wanted to save the message. I hit nine to save it and then continued to the next message.

"Got Rob home. He's trashed. I'm a little worried. I don't want to leave him yet just in case he falls or something. Be home as soon as I can." Another message from Genesis. That one had been at almost 3:00 a.m. last night.

The friend had been drunk. Extremely drunk, from what Gene said. Damn. Did that mean all the bruises and bite marks...?

My sight turned red with rage I hadn't felt in a long while. I approached the Park with scattered caution, a fight itching my skin. The air smelled of mischief. Hane had stalked my home all day, leaving his scent in the hall, mixing it across Gene's trail so I couldn't follow him. Tonight I needed someone other than my eccentric lover or his stupid friend to pulverize. Someone not human. A smile crossed my lips when a shadow fell into my path. Wish granted.

"About time you showed up. Too busy tucking lover boy in?" Hane leered at me, his black eyes hypnotizing.

"Cut the shit and start swinging." I threw my fist toward his face. He ducked, swung low, and doubled me over with the force of a truck slamming into my gut. A dark hand swept forward, coiling overly long fingers around my throat.

Air wasn't necessary; it just took longer for the brain to comprehend that and stop fighting to breathe. He smashed me into the ground hard enough to send stars flashing around my vision. Blood poured from my ears.

"Do you wish for a second death?"

"This time I'll take you with me." The metallic taste of blood trickled into my mouth. My blood was never as good.

"The boy has given you a new set of balls." His foot came down, crushing my chest, snapping rib bones and exploding pain into my heart. I battled the grip, but my fingers flowed over him like water. Michael had been like this in the end. Hane had never shown this dark side of power before. But then, he'd beaten Michael....

"I thought you wanted to die."

Why was I fighting? Was the brat really worth living for? Sure, the things he made me feel actually gave me a bit of my humanity back. And even though he pissed me off because those haunting eyes kept bringing back my past, something just came up missing without him. His voice was always in my head; I longed to pull musical sighs from his lips. "He's mine."

"Yet you let him go."

"It was a mistake."

"You make a lot of those where he is concerned." Hane gripped my hair and slammed my head into the pavement before pulling me up and dragging me out of the Park and toward boisterous noise.

Genesis

I FELL asleep around midnight tucked into Cris's king-size bed. Mikka slept curled beside me, purring and flicking her tail in contentment. She'd clung to me all night, even while I watched scary movies until the witching hour.

154

EVOLUTION

The graveyard dream returned, only the sunlight had vanished. I sat alone in the darkness, tombstones surrounding me like some mini forest of marble. The girl I usually saw had vanished. Her unnerving eyes always reminded me of KC, that liquid amber that saw right through me.

The ground beneath my feet began to move. And a hand broke through the earth, floundering, grabbing for something to hold on to. The watch on its wrist made me scream and jerk awake.

That had been KC's watch. He was sort of time obsessed, always looking at it.

Mikka stared at me with disdain for waking her, but I couldn't stay in bed with my heart hammering away and nightmares swirling in my head. What if KC was hurt? I pulled on a shirt and headed to my car. Even if he hated me, I had to make sure he was okay.

It took every last bit of willpower I had to obey the traffic laws. The ride took long enough for me to devise fifteen ways to explain my encounter with Rob last night without getting him killed or me dumped, though I admit to entertaining a few wishful visuals of KC beating the crap out of Rob. Kerstrande would understand. He had a lot of people fuck him over in his life, but he would believe me.

The condo was dark and empty when I arrived. Why I strode up expecting to find him sitting in on the couch, I didn't know. The door had even been unlocked. Was he hoping someone would break in?

I swiped my key from the counter. The girl ghost stood in the doorway to the bedroom looking somewhat amused. "Not home," she said.

"Thanks, Captain Obvious. Any idea where he went?"

"Out."

I groaned. "You're no help."

"Help you?"

"Not now!" I left, locking the door behind me, and headed to my next destination. The Park.

After sliding my crappy Honda in its usual spot, right next to KC's BMW, I jumped out and peered through the darkened windows of his car. He wasn't inside, not like I thought he would be, just checking....

I ran toward the bench, but it too sat empty.

The dark shadow of a person approached on the path. KC? But when he came into the light, I realized it was Hane.

"Sorry, kid. Not sure what you're looking for but didn't mean to disappoint." He reached out to pat me on the head, but I stepped back, fearing I'd fall apart if someone touched me. KC could be hurt somewhere. My stupid dreams did that sometimes—old me about bad things. Never enough to prevent any of it, though.

"Have you seen Kerstrande?" I asked Hane, praying he'd say yes.

He shook his head. "There's a party for a bunch of celebs going on. Maybe he stopped in after I left. It's really not my sort of party." Hane pointed. "Just a block or two down the road. Can't miss the noise."

"Thanks," I muttered before taking off in that direction. Something was wrong. I couldn't place it, didn't know where the trouble was coming from, but knew it had already been shot in our direction. The street didn't slow me down as I raced across it. Cars honked and the music got louder and louder as I approached.

A lot of people lingered in the street dressed goth-like in black clothes, chains, white face paint. I made my way through the crowd, its bright colors a solid wall to swim through, searching for any sign of KC. The smell of alcohol made my stomach queasy. When I entered the building, it felt like a fun house: oddities, mirrors, the stink of weed and sex. Some people danced, others did shots or drugs, some made out in groups, others looked like orgies of legs and arms flailing about.

A guy with long hair touched my arm. "Help you find something, Bit?"

"Kerstrande," I told him. "I'm looking for Kerstrande Petterson."

"Shame," he replied, then flicked his head in the direction of the stairs. "First door on the left."

"Thanks." I headed upward, fearing the worst. None of this seemed like KC's scene. His severely introverted, snarky nature would have him breathing scathing remarks and heading for the nearest exit. He'd never go to a party like this.

The door at the top of the stairs stood partially open. The room reeked of sex, pot, cigarettes, and blood. KC sat in the middle of a king-size bed, men and women moving around him like some sort of cocoon of flesh. Shadows covered his face. Blood smeared his lower jaw and bare chest, a clichéd horror movie come to life.

Did he see me standing right in front of him? Did he realize just how this moment stabbed like a dagger through my very soul? I turned from the scene and made my way back to the Park, numb, broken, and defeated.

I got into my car, not sure how I'd even made it there. Not that it mattered. When I turned the key, an explosion hit me with a wave of color, heat, and then silence.

CHAPTER 23

Kerstrande

MY WATCH stopped when the sound of an explosion rocked the entire building. Everyone froze, turning in unison toward the sound, but walls blocked the view. My stomach churned with the mix of blood in my gut. The bodies around me stank of sex, drugs, and unwashed flesh. I shoved the wall of bodies away from me. People yelped when they fell off the bed, but I'd never been so happy to find myself mostly clothed.

I stumbled for the door, buttoned my shirt, and pondered all the blood I'd had and the lingering ache in my bones. That's right, Hane had broken me quite thoroughly. Why would he want me to heal so fast?

At the top of the stairway, I caught Genesis's scent—incense and rain. He'd been here. Had he seen the corruption I'd been a part of? My head spun, nearly sending me tumbling down the stairs. I had to get to him. Explain, see if he would forgive me for not stopping him from leaving this morning.

The crowd moved in a mass exodus of vampires and groupies, dragging me along with them toward the Park. A mushroom cloud of smoke ballooned up from the parking area. Everyone stopped, keeping me farther back than I wanted. Was he there? Was Genesis okay?

I pushed my way through, letting them curse and glower. I got to the edge and saw the horror with my own two eyes. My BMW smoldered, damaged, but not nearly the twisted metal mess that had been the Honda parked next to it. The sirens and flashing lights of the police flashed like a strobe in my head, slowing down my world to a crawling speed.

The black smoke poured heavily from the car. No one could have survived that. The letters PG for Preservation Group flickered on the pavement two feet from the car, burning in gasoline.

I sunk to my knees, utterly destroyed. Maybe if I walked up to the cops right at this moment and proclaimed myself an illegal vamp, they'd let me jump in the burning car too. Finish me off. End me as surely as losing him would....

Genesis

THE graveyard again. Only this time there was no end to the darkness. The girl reappeared, took my hand, and walked with me for a while. Neither of us spoke, but it was a moment of complete contentment. I didn't feel dead, but nothing hurt, and my soul felt at peace. Odd. Especially if this graveyard of gray endless headstones was all I would get until I was born into my next life.

Kerstrande's betrayal felt so far away. Something about it all felt wrong. He would never have gone to that party on his own. I knew him well enough to know that. He went to the grocery store after midnight just to avoid other people. So what had happened? Finally I said, "Can you tell me anything?"

The girl turned my way and smiled, showing the dead part of her face as well as the radiant part. "Memories."

"Good ones or bad ones?"

"What do you choose?"

"KC."

"Even when he has hurt you?"

"I don't think it was his choice. Something wasn't right. That wasn't him."

She smiled again and kept walking, pulling me along with her. I had to pause when I suddenly felt our first kiss again. KC had breathed life into my life that day, awakened things in me I'd feared I'd never find.

It changed to him stumbling through the rain, feeding on three girls, having sex with them, but so completely blank-eyed I was sure he probably didn't remember what he'd done. Then the night he'd taken me from my flat and into his home. His panic when he'd finally become aware of his surroundings made my heart hurt. He'd feared he'd killed me, sat wrapped around me, weeping until I stirred in my sleep, probably from some dream I didn't remember.

"So he is a vampire," I whispered to the girl.

"He is eternal, just in a different way than you are."

Another vision appeared. This one was more horrific than the others, but it explained Michael Shuon's death. Michael turned into something really dark, a heap of shadows piled upon itself. It left a trail of dark ooze that killed the grass as he moved through it, stalking KC, who already dripped blood. Michael's hands changed, turning into claws or talons like an eagle might have. He flew across the distance to slam KC to the ground and tear into his back, slashing through the leather duster and his skin as easily as if it were paper.

KC's shriek of pain made my eyes begin to water. He responded with a blindingly fast turn to smash his fist like a hammer into Michael's face. Michael flew back, thudding against a tree, but spun around in some crazy martial arts move to meet KC's foot, which was raised to deliver a deadly kick. Michael twisted the caught leg. An audible crack sent KC tumbling to the ground, crying in agony.

EVOLUTION

Michael dropped the dislocated foot and hacked into KC, cackling like some madman in a horror movie. Then the motion stopped suddenly. Blood began to pour from the black heap that was Michael. It poured over KC's leg. He hissed and dragged himself away from the nasty flow.

Hane stood behind Michael, hand through the man's chest, gripping his heart. When he pulled the bloody pulp free, Michael should have been done, but he turned, a horror show of death and evil, and struck out at Hane. Hane returned his deadly slash with a swipe of some flashing steel. Michael's head toppled from his body, thunking to the ground like the dead weight it was.

KC crawled farther away while he watched Hane devour Michael's awful blood and then rip him apart. I felt KC's pain and wished I could touch him. He yanked his leg back into place, stifling the scream that wanted to break through. Tears clouded his vision. Not only had he lost Michael to the monster who'd been eating him slowly from the inside out for years, he would now watch the same thing happen to Hane. He wished he had never been changed, never given another life.

"It hurts him to be this way," I said, hating that I had to watch him in pain. "Isn't there a way to stop it?"

"Only when Yin meets Yang will you stop the cycle of destruction." Her words made more sense than anything else I'd heard so far. KC's aggression made him heavy with Yang. I remembered how often my grandfather told me of the necessity of balance. The question was, could I be KC's Yin? Was I enough to form a wall between him and that endless battle for his soul?

So much swam through my head, I began to feel a little dizzy and had to sit down. Something else she said finally clicked. "What do you mean I'm eternal? Do you mean like rebirth and stuff?"

"Yes, and yet no." She leaned down and kissed my forehead. "You should go."

"Huh?" I felt totally lost as her beautiful eyes expanded, filling the world around me. And then I was falling, plunging from the sky, the golden sun tinged with the red glow of a fading day. I sucked in a deep breath and flailed as the ground approached at a deadly speed. The wind seemed to catch me, letting me glide a way across the city. I flapped my wings, not understanding where I was for a few minutes, or better yet, what I was.

I felt like I was floating on a breeze so warm and gentle, a soul free of all bonds. Was this Nirvana? Had I achieved the ultimate in enlightenment? I soared above everything, a tug of some invisible bond leading me to swing in another direction.

A familiar form waved to me from below, offering a large, soft, white blanket in his arms for me to land in. I tumbled into that waiting embrace, felt the blanket wrapped around me, and was shoved into a car.

A wet nose dug through the folds of fabric before finally meeting mine. Mikka crawled in beside me and curled up around me, purring while she licked my feathers clean. It should have been odd to be smaller than Mikka, or to see myself covered in feathers, but I was too tired to care. I let the warmth of my furry companion's embrace lull me to sleep.

CHAPTER 24

I WOKE up in bed, wondering if it had all been a dream. Cris dozed beside me, arm wrapped around my waist, Mikka curled up near my head, still purring, tail flicking in happy tandem. The white blanket still covered my hips, but Cris lay on top of the blankets fully dressed except for shoes. Had he known? And how much did he know? Mikka had only come into my life after I'd met Cris that first time. So maybe he knew this was coming. Maybe even sent Mikka to me to care for me.

He stirred, opening sleepy eyes. Groaning, he tucked himself tighter against me, face buried against my neck. "It's too early, Gene. I'm a night owl, remember?"

"Like a real owl?"

He chuckled. The sound was warm and made me smile. "Nope. What you see is what you get."

I eyed Mikka, like maybe she was not telling me something. She just gave me a sleepy glare. "So what am I exactly?"

"Big questions first, eh? Meaning of life and all that?"

"I died. I turned into a bird. Was it all some sort of dream?"

"You didn't die. You were reborn." He grabbed the blanket from behind him and flung it over both of us, resulting in a startled mew from Mikka, who had to adjust her position. It also brought us closer. "You, my friend, are a phoenix."

The only memory I could place with the word was a kid's movie that had exploding birds with healing tears. How had I become this thing? My grandfather never mentioned anything, nor had my mother. Maybe they didn't know. Maybe my dad had been a phoenix too.

"I can see the wheels turning like crazy in your head. You're overworking your hamsters," Cris joked.

"How did you know I would change?"

"First time I touched you, your energy was off the chart. I could take all I wanted, and you'd just keep shrugging off more."

I turned toward him, disrupting Mikka even more, but facing Cris's rueful expression. "What are you?"

"You wouldn't recognize the word. Never were big on school." He brushed my hair out of my eyes. "I think I understand your lack of focus now. Having all that life flowing through you must keep you bouncing off the walls. My life is sex. Without sex I will wither and die." He shrugged. "Intimacy works too, but not as well as the real thing. It's how I knew that no matter how much I love you, you'll never be mine."

"I do love you." He was one of my best friends. Even if we weren't lovers anymore, I felt closer to him than most anyone.

"But you're not in love with me. I'm not enough of an opposite to balance you."

Rob had said something about me needing an opposite as well. "If I am life, what exactly is my opposite, then? Death?"

He sighed and yanked me into a hug. "Promise you'll remain my friend and come to me whenever you need."

"Of course. That's a dumb thing to ask."

He chuckled. "Not to me. I've been alone a long time. I was hoping you'd be my balance."

"I'm sorry." And I really was.

Cris ruffled my hair, then rolled away. He smoothed the blankets back in place and rounded the bed to scratch under Mikka's chin. "Twilight is falling. I have to go hunt. You should call your record label and your family to let them know you're alive. They think you're dead." He clicked on the TV, and the news filled the flat screen with images of my car, burned to a shattered hull, being towed away from the Park. "Best to not tell everyone what you are." Flickering flames that read "PG" filled the screen for a moment before firefighters put out the fire. "Not everyone appreciates those of us who are different." He vanished into the living room, and a moment later I heard the door open and close as he left.

I stared at Mikka, feeling so overwhelmed my thoughts were blank. Instead of facing the day, I just rolled over, pulled the blankets over my head, and tried to not feel overwhelmed by the past twenty-four hours of my life. Now I was on PG's radar, instead of just being a freak who saw things. I now changed into something weird, and KC had been involved in an orgy. Crap.

Tears filled my eyes. Oh no. I was so not letting this whole thing rip me apart again. So love didn't conquer all. Big deal. I'd lived this long just fine without it. I moved away from Mikka, ignored the messy bed, and stood in the middle of the bedroom thinking about the change I'd been through. Could I do it at will? I concentrated really hard, imagining I had feathers and could fly, but nothing happened. Dammit.

I picked up Cris's landline and called my mom. She responded with weepy joy when I told her I was alive and fine. She asked about the car, and I told her I had left it there to go for a walk but had found my way home instead of returning to it. It was only a partial lie, but I still felt awful about it. She made me promise to visit as soon as I could and to call my grandfather. The call to him was much the same. No one answered at the studio, and I didn't dare call Rob. So I threw on some clothes and headed down to hail a cab.

The ride went faster than I thought it would, mostly because I spent the whole time thinking about what to say. Truth was always easier to remember than lies. But the truth would likely get me killed. The time in the graveyard had reminded me of all the good times with KC, but being back in the real world made me mad just thinking about him with someone else. He'd never promised that he just belonged to me. Heck, he wouldn't even touch me other than an occasional kiss. What made me think he owed me anything? I sighed as the cab pulled up outside the studio.

The guard who let me in stared like he'd never seen me before. Did I look different? I hadn't had a chance to glance in the mirror. He radioed for Mr. Tokie, who appeared in the hallway just minutes later and wrapped his arms around me.

"We thought you were dead."

"I wasn't in the car. I went for a walk and then fell asleep. I came as soon as I heard the news." I gave him the same story I had told my family.

Rob appeared in the hallway behind him, as did a lot of the other staff, like my voice coach, and then a dark figure who made me forget to breathe for a few seconds.

"KC."

His eyes were wide as he stepped forward, moving past me, into the oncoming night. He paused at the door and turned back briefly, amber gaze falling to me, searching me from head to toe. I tried to keep the image of him with the wall of people around him out of my head. An odd mix of fury and sadness gripped my heart and locked me in silence.

Finally he said, "I'll give you a ride home."

Home? I didn't really have one. I suppose Cris's place was probably as close to home as I would get. "My home. Not yours."

His shoulders tightened. He exchanged a look with Mr. Tokie, nodded slightly to me, and then walked out the door, not waiting for me. Unease filled the hall. Rob's silent rage made me turn and follow

KC. I didn't need his anger today. I had enough of my own. Questions. Confusion. And sadly, heartbreak.

I slid in the passenger seat of Kerstrande's new car. He leaned over, snapped the seat belt into place, and started the car. Again we drove without the radio. At least the people at the studio had been happy to see me. They would spread the word that I was alive.

I glared out the window, not sure what to say, thinking maybe he should talk first but knowing he wouldn't. "Want to talk about the orgy?" I finally asked.

"No." The pain in his voice was unmistakable. I sighed.

"You cheated on me."

"That affects us how?"

"What us? Just take me home. *My* home." I rattled off the address. If he heard, I couldn't tell, but at least he seemed to be heading in the right direction. Was he just going to dump me there and vanish to lick his wounds again? "There *is* no us. You dragged me from my apartment in the middle of the night, dropped me at your place, only to break my heart with your silent accusations after my best friend tried to rape me. Then you offer to take me home after someone nearly kills me because you're a vampire trying to pretend not to be! And the home you're taking me to is not my home but the one I've borrowed from my only remaining friend because you destroyed mine!" I clutched the seat belt and fought not to look at him. "Why? You won't touch me. I just irritate you. Yet you keep dragging me back only to push me away again. Why do you care when you so obviously don't care?"

He said nothing but his hands tightened on the steering wheel. He pulled into the parking garage below the building but made no move to get out of the car. Everything about him said he wanted to rip the car apart and that still wouldn't make him happy. "Don't tell anyone," he finally said.

"I won't," I said, knowing he was talking about his secret vampirism. He might need to hide, but I didn't. In fact, I planned to be often photographed in the sunlight in front of churches if needed. I got out of the car. "Thanks for the ride."

He followed me upstairs, not speaking, not even walking beside me, just skulking behind. It made me want to scream, anything but exist in this vacuum of soundlessness. I fished the spare key out of my pocket and opened the door, not inviting him in. He stood in the doorway, leaning on the frame, staring at me like he wanted to say something but couldn't.

"What?" I finally demanded. "I'm here and safe. Go away. Go mess up someone else's life and leave me alone. It's what you're good at." A shadow moved across the bedroom door. Dammit. Now they were here too. At least this one had the lines of a human. These ghosts had to be KC's too, since I didn't have any of my own.

"What do you see?" Kerstrande asked.

My eyes flicked back to him. "Huh?"

"In me. What do you see in me? Why do you want me?"

"Are you kidding me?" I turned away. "Sometimes I don't know. You're mean. You don't treat me nice. But then sometimes you do. You smile and I feel like everything will be okay. And when you kiss me nothing else matters. But you don't want to kiss me."

"I do."

"Then why don't you?" I looked back at him, searching his face for answers.

"I'm not safe. People around me die."

"No kidding." I'd seen what Michael became and how Hane had taken him out. None of that was KC's fault.

"What do you see when you look at the bedroom? Me? Robert? Devon? Maybe your model friend, Cris?"

I sank to the floor at his feet. "You."

"And if I told you I wasn't interested?"

My heart would rip itself from my chest and batter itself on the floor until it was just a nasty little ball of flat, red goo. "Why? Why do you keep showing up in my life? Why would you say you want to kiss me, if you want nothing else?"

"Temporary lack of judgment."

"But it keeps happening." I hugged his legs. It was childish to beg, but I did it anyway. "Whatever you want, I can do it. I'll be better. I promise."

"Did Rob rape you?"

The words hit me like a fist in the gut.

"Why didn't you tell me he hurt you?"

"He tried but didn't succeed."

"But he did hurt you."

"Yeah." More than I ever thought possible.

That damned silence stretched again, until he said something I was never expecting to hear. "Do you want me to kill him?"

"No!"

He leaned down and kissed me on the lips. "How can you be so forgiving?"

"Death, murder, is not the answer."

"Your friend Joel killed his family."

My world flipped over trying to make sense of what he said. "Huh?"

"Sarah brought him over. Apparently he filled out the paperwork and everything needed to be registered as a vampire, but something went wrong. The cops in the city are looking for him, and if they find him it will be a public execution. To REA he is considered dead. And today we thought you were too." He hid his eyes behind his hair. "When I thought you were dead—"

"I'm not dead. PG—"

"Are denying the bombing. REA has released your health records to prove you're human. Hopefully PG will feel the backlash of this for a while. But they are denying having any part in it."

The reality fell into place finally. Joel was a vampire? He'd killed his parents? "Oh God. Joel killed people." And PG probably still thought I was a vampire.

"It happens to all vampires at some point. Control snaps. The older you are, the better control you have." Kerstrande sighed. "Mr. Tokie told me he'd replaced Joel at the studio with Hane a long time ago. I thought the tribute was just a one-time thing. You never told me that Hane was trying to force his way into the band."

We didn't talk about the music business because it made him grumpy. "Just like you haven't said anything about that orgy I saw you at."

"Hane beat me to a pulp. I think he put me there, not to heal, but to get caught by you."

"Hane?"

"He's my sire. He's the head of New York City. Oldest and most powerful vampire around, especially now that Michael is dead."

He'd never seemed like a bad guy when he'd been around me, but if he'd been hurting KC, he was not okay in my book. "He beat you up?"

"Many times. Fire him. Ban him from your presence. Pack your things. Come home with me, and I will give you everything you want from me."

Everything?

"Even sex."

I wanted much more than sex. "I fire Hane, and you'll be my boyfriend for real? You'll go on dates with me, kiss me, hold me, and make love to me?"

"Often."

My body reacted violently, but I stayed on the floor, face pressed to his thigh. "Can I say it now?"

He pulled away, heading toward the stairs. "Only if you need to."

"I love you, KC."

He stopped like I'd hit a button in him to turn him off.

"Do you love me?" I know it was asking for a lot.

"You ask too many questions. Complain too much. I'm giving you what you want. Yes, I will date you, be your lover. I'm not asking for much in return."

Just everything I was, but he already had all that. "I will fire Hane."

"Good. Go pack."

"You've bitten me, right? Will I turn into a vampire?"

"Takes more than one bite."

"How many times have you bitten me?"

Kerstrande stared at me now. "You're thinking. I can tell. It looks like it hurts you. You better stop."

I sighed. "You could be nicer to me you know. I almost died today." I would tell him when we got home. Everything, even what I became.

"You wouldn't like me nice." He disappeared down the hall toward the parking garage.

Probably true. I scrambled to gather up my things and made my way to the garage, Mikka in my arms. When I arrived downstairs, KC waited in the car.

CHAPTER 25

KERSTRANDE volunteered to make dinner. The idea of him cooking surprised me. How long had he been a vampire? I guess that's why there was so much boxed and canned food now. He'd bought those things for me.

"I need a bath. How long will dinner be?"

"An hour." He chopped vegetables.

I smelled like smoke, but I was sleepy. I didn't really want to shower, so I headed to his big bathroom and turned on the Jacuzzi. The water rushed in a heated bubbling flow to fill the tub. I stripped out of everything and relaxed onto the bench on one side. The hot jets eased my tight muscles. I laid my head back on the edge of the tub, where I'd placed a folded towel, and just let the heat do its work.

The door opened, waking me from a light, dozing sleep. Kerstrande stood in the doorway, expression unreadable.

"Is dinner done?"

He shook his head.

KC wore just jeans and a button-up pale-blue shirt. He looked so beautiful that I went from groggy to horny in two seconds flat. In just a few strides he crossed the room and sat on the steps connecting to the tub. He picked up a small cup and poured a bit of water over my head to wet my hair, careful not to get it in my eyes. "Let me wash your hair."

"Okay," I croaked out. He could wash any part of me he wanted to.

His hands massaging shampoo in my scalp could have been touching another part of my anatomy as strongly as my body reacted.

KC knelt beside the tub. Water seeped down his arms, wetting his sleeves and running down his shirt. I wanted to reach out and rip the buttons off, just to bare his chest to me. Would he let me touch him this time? Could I massage those strong shoulders, follow the lines of muscle down his back with my lips, and press the heat of my skin to his?

His face brushed mine, cheek to cheek, and then he turned my head his way and kissed me. Water splashed from the tub as I grabbed him and pulled him closer. If I could have crawled inside him while we kissed, I would have. He tasted of peppermint and that sweet metallic bite of copper. My hands spread bubbles and wetness all through his hair, which stood up on end.

We both broke the kiss at the same time to take a deep breath. His amber gaze bored into me from half-closed lids. Lust, oh God, that was lust for me! I jammed my mouth up against his again. He took it and gave the passion right back. My body almost seemed to sigh in relief that it was finally happening. KC was touching me. He was letting me touch him.

The stubble on his jaw made him look rough, and his lips were red from being kissed hard. I couldn't hold back from diving in for another kiss. If we never stopped kissing again, it wouldn't be long enough.

He let me go to rinse out the shampoo and massage the conditioner through my hair, from scalp all the way to the tips. Each stroke of his long fingers made my nerves sing. Gritting my teeth, I tried to think of things like baseball games or tea with my grandpa.

"KC, you're killing me," I told him when he finished with my hair.

He chuckled lightly, the vibration against my back too much. I couldn't hold back. My face filled with the heat of embarrassment.

"Sorry."

"It's okay." He grabbed a towel and dried my hair. Was it over so soon? "You've got whisker burn."

I touched my face. The skin was a little tender. "I'm okay with that."

KC crossed the room and pulled an old-fashioned shaving kit out of the drawer. He stared in the mirror, obviously seeing only the stubble and not himself since he didn't seem to do more than raise his chin from side to side and trail his long fingers over his neck and Adam's apple. Everything about him was so sleek and perfect.

"Can I do it?" I heard myself ask before I even realized what I was saying.

He raised a brow at me in the mirror. His shirt was soaked, and the knees of his pants were wet. Maybe I could strip him down and have my way with him. I shut off the water and carefully stepped out.

KC mixed up some shaving cream and began patting it over his face. I moved a chair over and pushed him into it.

"Do you even know how to do this?"

"It's not like you're using an actual knife to shave. I've used razors before." Not that I'd ever had anything but peach fuzz. My Asian heritage ensured that my hair was fine and that I had very little body hair. "I kind of like you scruffy."

"And how much makeup will the studio have to put on you to cover up the redness?"

I carefully began to pull the razor in long strokes over his skin, dumping off the cream into the sink. "I wish I didn't have to go to the studio every day to sing. But I bet you like seeing me in makeup."

He said nothing, but I felt his cheeks move a little, like he was smiling beneath all that white foam. Shaving him was a bit like a dream. His foot caressed my bare hamstring, and I stood between his legs to get close enough to keep a good grip on the razor. The proximity gave me another woody, but just as before he didn't seem to notice, though he did watch me in the mirror.

Each stroke of the blade made me harder. I sighed, leaning against him and trying not to hump his leg. Embarrassment burned my face, but his sweet little smile made it all worth it. When I finally washed the last of the foam away with a damp cloth, the grin was unmistakable.

"Why are you smiling so much?" It was starting to worry me.

"You're very young."

I frowned. "So? You're what, a year older than me?"

"You done?" He ran his hands over his cheeks, feeling the smooth skin.

"Yeah."

"Good." He jumped up from the chair, grabbed me up in his arms, and headed to the bedroom. I couldn't think of any protests, not that I would have anyway.

CHAPTER 26

KERSTRANDE and I only got out of bed briefly so he could feed me the wonderful dinner he'd made me. I really liked this boyfriend KC instead of the grumpy resistive KC, though I was aware they were one and the same. Mr. Grumpy would be back eventually. The phone ringing brought me out of sleep early the next morning.

"Not now." Kerstrande's phone again. "I already made myself clear on the matter."… "No."… "He's fine."… "That's all I have to say." The phone clicked off, and there was a thud as it hit the floor. He rolled over and wrapped his arms around me again. I peered at him over the heap of pillows. If he was going to be cuddly, I wasn't about to pull myself out of bed. Even if it meant being late for work.

KC glanced my way and frowned. "What?"

Like I'd dare ask anything. "Morning." Would he push me away if I kissed him? Instead I ran my hands across his smooth face. "I need to tell you what happened to me yesterday."

"Okay." And so he listened. Emotions crossed his face too fast for me to read, but I kept going until the very end. He blinked at me for a few minutes, probably trying to process the strange thing I was. Would he kick me out now?

"Should I leave?" I finally whispered.

EVOLUTION

"No."

"Are we okay?"

He leaned in and stole a kiss, then whispered in my ear. "You'll tell Hane today, right?"

I nodded, unable to find my voice with him so close. Last night had been everything I'd hoped for since our relationship began. If only we could keep it moving in the right direction. His hand smoothed over my stomach, going lower and lower. I had to swallow back my groan.

"You need to eat. Keep up your strength for tonight." He rolled away then, scooting to the edge of the bed and shoving his long legs into a pair of jeans. I wished he wasn't so eager to leave me for the day, but I did have to get to work. KC didn't look back when he left the room in search of coffee.

A deep sigh escaped me when he left. It took me another fifteen minutes to pull myself free of the warmth and smell of him all over the blankets. When I finally got dressed, I added one of KC's sweaters over my T-shirt since the overcast sky predicted rain. When I entered the kitchen, he handed me a mug of coffee but only glanced at me. The corners of his lips turned up a bit, but he hid his smile behind his cup.

"Is there any hope for Joel?" I had to ask.

"Depends on what you mean. If the cops catch him, no. Even if he found a mentor who could control him, he may have transitioned from human to vampire wrong. In that case, killing him would be a mercy."

"Would you be strong enough to control him?"

"If Sarah couldn't, then no. I'm a baby in vampire terms." He set his cup down and refilled it. The coffee sat in my stomach like oil, heavy and painful. Was it my fault Joel had been turned? How could he have agreed to it?

"Was it my fault?"

KC hugged me briefly, then let go. "No. He was already in the scene. Liked to be bitten. Or so I heard."

The idea made me shiver. What would we do now? Joel was part of Evolution. So was Rob, but I wasn't sure we would ever be the same. Just thinking of Rob made me remember what he'd tried to do to me. "I dread singing some days." Even more so now that I seemed to be all alone.

"There are ways out of the contract," KC said.

I had to look at him. "Huh?"

"If you're really unhappy, there are ways out of the contract." He pulled a stack of cash out of his pocket. "Cab fare. Be back early. It's not safe to be out after dark."

"Because of vampires?"

"Because a lot of people do bad things under the cover of a night sky." He set the paper on the counter, and today's news was more attacks on vampires. There was another story about a Hindu Temple that had been vandalized overnight too. But the headline read, "Evolution Singer Found Alive?" It went on to question my humanity, even showing medical records, which I thought were private, and how I had some hyperactive white blood cells. Guess privacy didn't exist if you're a singer signed with a major label. PG even made a statement about how they hadn't been part of the explosion, but that my existence was in question. *Sigh.*

I finished my coffee and then slid into my shoes, thinking about the contract. Would there be a way to be released from it and leave Rob something? Maybe he could be a studio musician. That would be closer to his goal, even if he didn't have his own band. He just didn't have to be around me.

"You're thinking again," Kerstrande pointed out.

I smiled and crossed the room to peck him on the lips before heading to the door. The truth was, thinking about it all was hurting me, and KC had a point. "I'll try not to think so much."

"Make quick work of your business today, and I'll have you in bed by noon. You won't be doing any recording without Joel or Hane."

EVOLUTION

I blushed my way out of the apartment and down to the street to get a cab. Another night like last would be nice. The sooner I could get to the studio and fire Hane, the faster I could make my way home. Maybe Mr. Tokie knew something about the contract. Would he be willing to help if I wanted out?

At the studio, I couldn't find Rob or Hane, but Mr. Tokie was in his office. He waved me in. "Hello, Genesis, you have the day off. REA is doing some media cleanup. Did Kerstrande tell you about Joel?"

"Yeah." Not that I really believed he'd killed his parents. That blame belonged to whoever changed him. Hadn't KC implied it was Sarah? She was a vampire? That explained a lot, didn't it? I took a deep breath and then let it out, more nervous than I thought I'd be just for asking. "I wanted to ask you about my contract."

"Sure. What sort of questions do you have?"

"Is there an out?"

He blinked at me for a few moments. "Do you want to change the contract? Or just not work for REA?"

"I want to sing. I just don't want to be told that my songs suck. Sure, they need some polish. But I wrote most of 'Midnight Rain'. Kerstrande just changed the score up a bit." He'd walked in on one of our practice sessions last week and gushed over how great "Midnight Rain" was. I took another deep breath. A lot of things had changed since last week. Was I really going to cut Rob out of my life? "I also don't want to work with a band anymore." Rob and I were no longer friends, and KC wanted Hane gone. I could work with studio musicians if needed. "I understand if I'm not good enough to stand on my own, but I can no longer work with Rob. And Hane was never meant to be a permanent part of the band. He's just not a good fit. Without Joel and Rob, there is no Evolution."

"Did something happen between you and Rob?"

Yes, but I wasn't going to broadcast it. "We just have personal and professional differences of opinion. We are not moving in the same direction." That was about as neutral as I could play it.

Mr. Tokie smiled. "You are very young. Things often change as you get older. Friendships and alliances are lost and found. Sometimes old ones are reforged."

No kidding. "I just want to sing and not be ridiculed by my label or a bandmate. I'm sure the world at large will give me enough of that. Can you make that happen?"

"Maybe. However, you're suggesting some pretty big changes. You can probably change the members of the band. Being the vocalist always has advantages in that regard. As it stands right now, it is binding to keep you in the band and produce at least one full album as Evolution. If that sells well enough, they may offer you just a solo contract. The board holds the reins."

I sighed. Whoever the rich shareholders of our contract were, it was unlikely they'd listen to me. Squabbles aside, I could make music if I had to. It was becoming just a job. Maybe I could make it one I liked better. "Is my being gay going to be an issue?"

"Only if you make it one."

How was it my fault if people had an issue with it? "What does that mean?"

"It means as long as you keep out of trouble, no one cares."

"But you're not going to make me pretend to be straight to continue to work for REA?"

"We don't believe in discrimination." He pulled out a file that had several copies of articles written about Evolution. "As for your personality, everyone seems to like you. We have calls every day for interviews. Your look could use some polishing too, but it seems that a lot of teens today like what they see."

Well, that was a relief. "Can we at least change the music? You like 'Midnight Rain'. I have more like that."

"You want to trash all the work you've done so far?"

"It's not me. Not even me singing my best. I'm willing to work harder to get the new stuff done in the same amount of time if necessary."

"If you can get Kerstrande to look at the rest of your songs and approve them for production, then I'm okay with throwing out what you've already done. Except for 'Midnight Rain'. That song is going to be your first single."

"I will ask him." I couldn't promise, simply because KC did what he wanted when he wanted, but I could ask. "Are you okay with me not working with Hane anymore?"

"We're already looking for another keyboardist. Hane was never meant to be permanent. Evolution and Triple Flight are very different groups. I would prefer you move down different paths as well."

Did he know they were vampires? Is that what he meant? "I'd like to tell Hane myself, if that's okay. Is he here today?"

"That's fine. But no, he's not here. He stopped in earlier and then headed home." He took a notebook out of his pocket and jotted down an address. "If you see Joel anywhere, run the other way. Don't talk to him, just call the police. You understand how dangerous he is, right?"

"Yes." When had I become such a good liar? If Joel approached me, I'd have to try to talk to him. I took the address from Mr. Tokie. "Thank you so much," I said, bowing my head to him. His smile was amused as I raced for the door. Maybe he didn't hate me as much as I thought.

Going to Hane's home knowing he was a powerful vampire and KC's sire probably should have put me more on edge, but he was also hiding what he was, so I wasn't all that worried. He lived in an old brick building that appeared to have appeared to have been a factory at one time. The windows across the side of the building glared outward like black eyes. There were no signs of decorations or flowers or any of the normal things people often do to make their home more appealing. Perhaps vampires didn't feel the same need to decorate.

I rang the bell and waited. Maybe Hane just really hated the press. If they got too close they might discover his secret. I guess I wouldn't want anyone peering in my windows either. What if they saw me change into a bird? Not that I really knew how that happened.

I buzzed the bell again.

"Come in, Genesis," Hane's tired voice finally said as the door clicked open. I pulled it and stepped inside to an almost black darkness. In the dim light I could make out a spiral stairway leading up and a large metal grate blocking one that went down. At least I was alone. No living or dead lingered. I headed up the staircase. Three solid turns and finally the top step led to a door. The door creaked open before I was close enough to touch it. The heat of a fire hit me. Sure it was cold out, but not cold enough to have a fireplace burning that hot.

The actual hearth took up a good part of the room. The rest of the room stretched wide with concrete floors and very little furniture. Hane relaxed on an old-fashioned couch, blanket pulled up around him. He didn't look right, pale and almost sick. How was that possible? Vampires didn't get sick, did they?

"Are you okay?" I couldn't help but ask.

"Does it matter? You came to fire me, right?"

What the hell? Could he read my mind?

"Yes, I can. Kerstrande has some balls to send you here alone."

"He didn't send me. I thought you'd be at the studio. Mr. Tokie gave me your address. I told him I wanted to tell you myself. You're not right for the group anyway. We don't want to be vampires." Just how dangerous was Hane? Sure he'd killed Michael, but something had been wrong with Michael, and he'd tried to kill Kerstrande. "Why did you hurt Kerstrande?"

"Because I like to." He laughed at my expression. "Not what you wanted to hear, I know. But it's the truth."

I sighed and turned toward the door. I was so done here. There were enough sadistic assholes in my life.

"Don't you want to see your friend?"

EVOLUTION

"Friend?"

Hane threw the blanket off and got up from the couch. His smile made me think of someone who could kill puppies with no remorse. "I'm sure Joel will be thrilled to see you. He's certainly been lacking in visitors."

My whole world seemed to stop. "Joel? He's here?"

Hane led me to the stairs, down and to the locked gate. "Bottom of the stairs, through the door and to the left. He's chained to the wall, so don't worry." He opened the gate and motioned me inside.

The darkness was thicker here. The door at the bottom of the stairs opened easily enough, but it was heavy, metal maybe? The smell of blood hit me the second the door swung outward. Was he hurt? Oh God. "Joel?"

Nothing. It was warm down here too. The air was stale. Maybe there were no windows? A maze of halls spanned out from the door. I turned left and passed many open, barren rooms. The one at the end was closed. Was that where I'd find Joel? A single sconce flickered pale light in an almost monstrous glow. The metal of this door was more like something out of a prison: heavy steel frame, a small window to look through, and a large handle that rolled a bar lock into place.

I had to use all my weight to get the handle to move, but the door finally creaked open. The smell nearly knocked me flat. Not blood this time, but filth. Oh God.

"Joel?" The light fell on his face, and he cringed away. Chains rattled. I stepped inside to try to see him better. "Joel?"

He growled an inhuman sound at me, and the sound of metal grinding almost made me put my hands over my ears. He must have moved closer because the stench increased. I stepped back, retreating to the room entrance. Maybe there was another light somewhere? Water, even. I could help him, treat him better than the animal that they made him out to be.

"He's hungry," a voice said from behind me.

I spun around to face Hane. "Crap!"

He smiled, looking ghoulish in the harsh light. How did everyone not see though him?

"Is there a way to get more light in here? Water, maybe? It smells awful. You can't treat him like this." You can't treat anyone like this and expect them to be human after they came out.

"He didn't come over right. None of this matters to him." Hane leaned over and touched something on the wall that made the room erupt into bright light. Fluorescents overhead buzzed to life. The room was little more than a ten by ten box. No windows, just the door, a mess of human excrement and blood, and a friend chained to the floor.

Joel's keening cry made me cringe. I didn't want to look at what he'd become, but I had to. He needed someone to care for him, and he'd always cared about me. The once self-confident ladies' man huddled over his knees, clothes torn ragged and stained. His skin had an awful white pallor that must have meant death. Though he still had yet to look at me, I knew he and Kerstrande were a billion times different.

"Water?" I finally asked, knowing Hane hadn't left.

"He can't drink it."

"But he can be washed. Did you keep Kerstrande down here, tied up like an unwanted dog too?" My anger built wave upon wave as I examined the conditions of this cage. The silence that responded to my question was worse than a resounding yes. How long had he kept KC here?

"Until he would kill."

Monster.

"Yes."

"Stay out of my head," I yelled at him. He stood so close I should have felt fear, but there was nothing but the rage. "Get me water or get out."

He stepped back. "The door on the right leads to a bathroom and a cleaning closet. Light switch on the wall. Come back up when you want out." He vanished down the hall while I made my way to the bathroom. A full bucket of water and some mostly clean rags would be a good start. The only soap was an antiseptic hand soap. Better than nothing, I guess.

I returned to the room, dragging the bucket of suds-filled water. Joel was testing his chains. His feet, hands, and neck were all bound. Dark black bruising bloomed from around each link. Obviously it hurt him, but he still yanked at them. The floor was stained with dried blood and other things. I sighed, got a mop, and began to clean. No point in cleaning him up until his surrounding "cage" was clean.

After a while, Joel stopped straining against the chains and sat down to watch. His eyes looked so blank and empty. His playful light was gone. Was there anything left of my friend? His blond hair stood up in many areas, streaked with dried blood. His eyes looked huge and shattered, his face like something out of a zombie movie, minus the whole brains-dripping-off-his-face thing.

Once the floor around him was clean, I approached him with a bit more caution. He backed away as far as the chains would allow, but I couldn't let myself forget that he was a vampire now. Kerstrande never showed me that side of himself. He was always in such control. But they could kill. I'd watched Hane tear Michael into little pieces with his bare hands.

Joel seemed so lost, his aura dim, but none of those shadows seemed to have him yet. I wondered if he would attack me? Hane said he was hungry. Did that mean he'd been purposely starved? Was Hane setting me up to be murdered by my friend?

Too late to back out now. Joel needed me. I shook all the thoughts out of my head and got back to work. Was there anything else for him to wear? He was not going to continue to sit in those rags. He'd probably been wearing them for weeks. The Joel I knew would be humiliated.

Returning to the bathroom, I dumped the bucket, washed it out, and refilled it with clean water. When I approached him this time, he didn't cringe away; instead he just stared at me, eyes wide. Maybe he recognized me.

"Hey, Joel. Let's get you cleaned up, okay?" I washed his face first, scrubbing gently at the pale lines that ran down his cheeks. They looked like tearstains, and after I washed the dirt away, he seemed a little better. He let me squeeze the water over his head and even squirt some soap in his hair. I didn't care much about the water ruining his clothes. I'd burn them later if possible. It just seemed so important to make him human again, even if he never would be.

"We've really missed you in the band. Rob did some things... unforgivable things." But then, everyone said Joel murdered his parents. If attempted rape wasn't forgivable, how could murder be? I sucked in a deep breath. My grandfather would have said that all things in this life prepare us for the next. Nothing was really a sin, not like in Christian theology; it was just bad Karma. Some things weighed more than others, kept us from progressing. Good karma did the opposite. Perhaps. Even if others weren't able to forgive the things they had done, they could still get closer to enlightenment, peace, acceptance, in another life. Maybe I could help Joel find a better path. Hane said he'd come over wrong. I wasn't sure what that meant, but maybe I could help him. Fix whatever was broken. I could at least try. That was more than everyone else seemed willing to do.

When I reached across to pull off his shirt, he sunk his teeth into my arm with an ease of biting into a tomato. It stung, but I didn't dare pull away. His teeth would have shredded my skin. He sucked on the wound, licking at any escaping blood. I sat back and just let him drink for a while. Who knew how long Hane had starved him? Only when I started to feel a little light-headed did I pull away. Joel still clung tight.

"Hey, let me go now. You've had enough," I told him with soft words. He glanced at me only briefly but didn't loosen his hold. Panic began to set in. What if he killed me? He wouldn't mean to—he didn't seem to understand anything I said—but I felt heat rising in my blood. Would I change? Somehow I didn't think that would help Joel or myself. "Stop!"

EVOLUTION

His grip let go, and he flinched away like a battered dog. I used one of the last dry rags to bandage the wound and went to work undressing him, cutting most everything off, and washing him. He sat docile now, unlike I'd ever known Joel to have been, while I bathed him head to toe, even scrubbing the chains that bound him. He didn't try to attack again, though my neck was bared and close to him. I must have been down there for several hours, but it passed so fast I barely noticed. At least the place didn't look so much like a prison for someone to be left to die in. And Joel, while still pale, didn't seem nearly as dead now that he was clean and functioning off of my blood.

"Still alive down here?" Hane asked suddenly from the doorway. "I'm surprised. He's slaughtered anyone I've brought to him in the last week. Made a total mess out of eating. More blood on the floor than in him."

"I want to take him home with me."

Hane's laugh was sharp and bitter. "Kerstrande would kill him the second he arrived. But maybe you like the murderous side of your boyfriend."

"At least undo the chains so I can tend his wounds."

"He'll heal."

Not under Hane's care, dammit. "He's my friend."

"I'll tell your boyfriend that when he shows up to claim your corpse." Hane stalked across the room and unlocked the chains. The last link clunked to the ground, and Hane moved across the room too fast to see, then stepped out the door and slammed it shut. "Pound when you want out," he said into the panel in the door then slammed it shut, laughing as he walked away.

Joel and I faced each other with him hunched on his heels, staring at me with an odd expression. I shrugged off my sweater and pulled it over his head. He didn't seem to remember how to wear it, but it covered him nearly to his knees. I suppose it was good he only had two inches on me. Kerstrande wouldn't mind that I lent out his sweater. I hoped.

How often did new vampires need to feed? Crap, I had to be able to do more than this for him.

There was a cot in the corner, tipped over and thrown around. I set it right, but the linens were dirty. I sighed. At least the mattress looked fairly clean. "Come here," I told Joel, patting the mattress. After a moment, he inched forward, finally coming to a stop beside me in front of the bed. "Aren't you tired?" I asked him.

He raised a hand, and I thought for a moment he meant to hit me, but he touched my hair, in fact seemed to be petting it.

"Are you okay?" I whispered to him.

He sighed and sat down on the bed, then lay back, putting his face to the wall. I went to the door and pounded on it. Hane took a good ten minutes to answer. He stood like a wall in front of me, eyebrow raised.

I shoved the dirty blankets at him. "Clean linens?"

He threw them outside the door and stepped back to point at a small door beside the bathroom I hadn't noticed before. Inside were clean blankets and pillows. I dug out a stack and brought them to Joel, covered him with the blanket to his chin, and tucked a pillow beneath his head.

"Be good," I whispered to him. "When Hane tells you to drink, just take a little, and don't kill anyone else, okay?"

Joel blinked at me but seemed to have heard. I headed for the door.

"Taming the beast, eh?" Hane said as he pulled the door shut behind us and relocked it. "He'll tear that room apart again in a few hours."

"He's not an animal."

Hane pressed his face in close to mine, his dark eyes seeming to glow in the once again dim lighting. He snapped off the light switch for the room. "We are all animals, kid. Some of us just have visible fangs."

"I'll be back for Joel. And stay away from Kerstrande. He's mine." I turned my back on him and stomped back to the main stairway and up to the gate. Letting a vampire have my back probably wasn't the smartest thing I could do, but I really wanted to hurt him. Some things were worth the bad karma. I just didn't have that kind of power. At least not yet.

Hane grabbed my arm in a nearly bone-crunching grip. "Maybe you should stay. Since you're giving out blood today."

"Not to you."

"I don't think you have a choice." He backed me against the wall. "Michael wanted you. That's why he engaged Kerstrande in a fight. Kerstrande doesn't like to share, but to kill Michael meant taking on the monster inside of him. Your cowardly boyfriend couldn't do it, so I had to." Hane's eyes flickered with some other personality, and blackness began to enshroud him. "He eats at me now. Telling me to take you, rip out your throat, and display your insides for Kerstrande to see."

"But you won't."

"What's to stop me?" He yanked my head to one side, baring my neck.

I smiled, letting the heat that had been building come to the surface with my anger. Was that how it worked? His hand on my arm began to smoke, and his expression changed to one of pain.

"Powerful little shit," he said but didn't release me. "No wonder Petterson has it so bad for you. Like fucking a volcano, I bet."

His teeth grazed my neck when I felt the anger rise up in me with the force of a wrecking ball. He wanted to do this just to hurt Kerstrande. I was just a means to an end. But I wasn't about to be another hanger-on to hurt KC.

A red glow flowed around my skin. My hand seared into his chest where I was pushing him away, filling the hallway with the stench of burning flesh. He screamed and shoved me away, hard enough to send me flying several feet. I sucked in a heavy breath and felt the fire surrounding me.

Hane rolled around the ground, screaming and flailing. The fire grew in intensity while I stared at him and let my anger free, thinking about how he had treated KC. It was Joel's face, peering through the tiny open slat in his door that made me reel back and stop. His eyes were wide, fearful. My heart pounded, but the fire stopped as though I'd just turned it off. What had I done?

CHAPTER 27

THE ride home in the cab took forever because traffic was backed up. I kept thinking about the look in Joel's eyes and how it felt to burn Hane when he threatened me. What was I becoming?

It was just after two in the afternoon when I arrived home. KC was curled up in bed, blankets wrapped around him. I slipped off my shoes and crawled in beside him. The room was dark as usual, the window covered, but I didn't mind just seeing the outline of his face. His beauty couldn't be masked by even the blackest of days. How had I been so lucky to deserve him?

"You're thinking again," Kerstrande grumbled into his pillow.

"It's not hurting me. I'm thinking about you."

"What a waste of time."

I laughed at his tone.

"You dye your hair again?"

"No."

KC rolled over and flicked the bedside lamp on. "It's red. Like blood red." He frowned at my hair.

I tugged my hair around so I could see it, and sure enough it was dark red with a tinge of orange. A color I'd never managed to get in many attempts at dyeing it. "Crap, and you like the blond."

He shook his head. "I don't care what the fuck color your hair is as long as it's still attached to you."

Had he really just said that? My heart skipped a beat, and I felt my smile get huge. I threw myself into his arms. "I fired Hane."

"And you survived. I'm not surprised."

I pouted. "Did you think he'd hurt me?"

"No. He saves the torture for me." KC settled us back onto the bed and let his forehead rest against mine. "You would just be a way to hurt me."

Because KC cared about me, even if he wasn't ready to admit it. "I love you, KC."

"So you keep telling me." But he was smiling when he said it. He ran one hand through my hair while the other cupped my butt, keeping me comfortably within his grasp.

"I told Hane he can't have you. You belong to me. And since I burned him by accident, he probably won't be coming my way anymore."

"Burned him?"

I sighed and tried to look anywhere but at his amber eyes. "I got really mad, and the fire just came out of me. He was demanding to feed on me 'cause he knew it would bug you. I said no. He wasn't taking no for an answer." Finally I met his gaze. He appeared amused, not angry or worried. "You really don't like Hane, do you?"

"I used to. The last of that died in me when he killed Michael." KC looked stricken for a second, then seemed to decide to let it pass. I hadn't told him the part about when I died and had been reviewing memories that were both his and mine.

"I knew about that. Saw it when I died in the car and was reborn. The girl with your eyes showed me."

KC tilted my face up to look at me again. "What girl? You didn't say anything about a girl before."

"She looks like you, only she's a girl, and part of her face is dead. The other part's normal."

He just looked confused.

"I'm sorry," I said automatically. Sometimes my oddities were just too much for people.

"She looks like me? Maybe that's why you're so obsessed, longing after this girl…."

"I think you have me confused with some other guy with red hair, 'cause I really like boys and all their wonderfulness." I let my hand slide between us to cup his crotch. "Especially this grumpy guitar genius with a killer body and lots of money." The girl and I never talked about her. She was just there sometimes and not the rest of the time. "When we talk, we talk about you. I've seen her since I was a kid. Most of the time we don't talk at all."

"That makes no sense." He pulled away and perched on the edge of the bed. I wrapped my arms around him from behind, hugging him to let him know I was there. It was the least I could do. "Maybe she's a ghost. What other ghosts are following me?"

"You believe me now?"

"I've always believed you. Why you stay with me when you see what I really am, I have no idea."

"You're beautiful."

He rolled his eyes.

"Handsome?" I tried.

"Whatever."

"We're meant to be together."

"Now I know you're crazy."

Sigh. His self-depreciation made me want to kick him. "You're hot, and a rock-legend with buckets of money."

"That I believe."

I shook my head at him. "The rest will just have to come with time."

He shrugged.

"I need to tell you something."

"You already said you love me."

"Yeah, and I do. But something happened at Hane's."

His mood turned black at the mention of his sire's name. "What did that bastard do this time?"

"I saw Joel." I needed to tell him, even if he was angry. "Hane has him locked up in a cell like some animal. I don't want him to stay with Hane. And if you say Joel can't stay here, I'll bring him to Cris's place and stay there with him until he's better."

"Better? He's a vampire. He's not going to get better. It doesn't go away. It just slowly eats away at you until there's nothing left that's human."

"He can at least be like you—able to live around other people, function as a person. He is still a person, even if he has a disease."

KC sighed and pushed me away. "No matter what science and the media tell you, it's not a disease any more than you being able to see the dead is a disease. You just are, or you aren't. Vampirism is magic, pure and simple. You won't catch it by having sex with me. You won't even catch it if I bite you. I have to want it. You have to want it, and you have to die to get it."

"So you're telling me Joel wanted to be an animal? You wanted to be an animal? Hane had him sitting in a nasty blood-and-feces-filled room. I wouldn't even treat a killer dog that way." I loved that he was talking to me, actually revealing things, but also feared the breakdown he might bring upon himself. KC wasn't really good at facing hard truths.

"I never wanted this." He stared at his hands as though they were malicious appendages. "An animal is what we are. We try to fit in, but we are just animals in disguise."

I pressed my cheek to his, ignoring the awkward angle, just needing to be close to him. "You're not an animal or a monster. You are KC, my boyfriend." I loved the word, though it sounded so high school and I was supposed to be past all that since dropping out. "I've seen some of the things you do. You don't remember them."

"Because I'm wrong. Something breaks in me when I don't feed. The monster comes out."

"So we just have to keep you fed, that's all." His face felt cool against mine. I was happy he didn't push me away again. This time when I moved, I gave him some space, got off the bed, and decided since I was staying home, I'd go a little more casual. I stripped off my clothes, stole the button-up shirt he'd tossed off before bed from its place on the floor, and slung it over my shoulders. Yeah, it was a little big for me. But it smelled like KC.

He just stared. I smiled and strode from the room, intending to make some coffee. I couldn't sleep all day, even if I wanted to.

In the kitchen, I made ramen, standing at the counter waiting for the noodles to soften in the steamy bowl while I wore nothing but KC's shirt. I sort of hoped he'd come into the kitchen and attack me. He'd left the bedroom to perch on the couch, watching me. He glanced my way a half dozen times, nostrils flared, eyes heavy-lidded. But he hadn't moved from his spot on the couch.

I flicked the radio on, pulled the plate off the bowl of steaming ramen, and stirred the noodles. The tune that played was something with a good beat I couldn't help but dance to. The soup was good and filling. I finished it, put the dish away, and kept moving to whatever came next. KC's eyes followed every move, bringing a smile to my lips. He could pretend I didn't do anything for him, but that was a lie.

He moved so fast I didn't hear him get up from the leather sofa. Suddenly he was there in front of me, backing me against the wall. His weight slid against me, hands pressing the shirt open so he could touch my bare body. He dropped his hands low, cupping my ass and grinding his hips against mine. I sighed just inches from his lips, wanting nothing more than for him to kiss me.

"You don't know what you do to me," he whispered.

I had a pretty good idea since he was hard against my hip. "I fired Hane," I reminded him.

KC licked my collarbone, nipped it lightly, and then blew on it before repeating the cycle. "Oh God."

"Yeah," I agreed, moving my hips against him, not caring that he was fully dressed and I mostly naked. "Please, KC."

"You have no idea what you're asking for."

Yeah, I did. "Just you, KC. All I need is you."

He laughed, a deep rumble that pressed us so intimately together I nearly came. "I totally believe you're some kind of incubus."

"Nope, just some goofy fireproof bird who sees dead people." Cris was the incubus. I'd looked it up online after he told me. "You, on the other hand, are some kind of legend, and I don't just mean of the musical kind."

His lips met mine. When he finally released the kiss, we were both breathing heavily. "God…."

"Hmm," was all I could reply. Words had no place for moments like these.

CHAPTER 28

THE next day, Mr. Tokie picked me up, and I happily handed him a stack of new music KC had approved. After several bouts of mind-blowing sex I found KC was pliable to just about anything I asked. But he'd stolen all my thunder when he'd dropped a stack of remixed songs in my lap. Apparently he'd been working on them since he'd found my orange notebook. A fresh book sat with my key on it beside the door, the inside cover filled with KC's scrawl: "Genesis's Songbook."

I was thrilled to be back at the studio for the first time in ages. At least now I could be me, play the music that meant something to me, and not just popular crap some random person sent my way. My vocal coach helped with five out of the stack, spending most of the day mastering the melody with me and pushing me to add more passion to the songs. She had me singing with tears streaming down my face or struggling not to laugh. And I couldn't have been flying higher until a familiar dark shadow stepped into the practice room.

It should have been Rob since I hadn't seen him all day—and really didn't want to—but it was Devon. He stood there staring at me, looking very much like he'd walked out of the pages of a pop magazine centerfold. He gave my voice coach a minor smile. "Can I talk to Gene for a few minutes, Lauren?"

She nodded and left us alone. When the door closed, it felt a lot like a prison cell door had slammed shut. The man before me didn't much look like the man I'd first met a few years ago. That man had been smiling, filled with light, and ready to teach a newbie like me the ropes. This man was shrouded in shadows and pain.

"Hey, Devon."

He moved toward me, hand outstretched as though to touch my face. I stepped away. He stopped and frowned. "I spoke to your manager, and the papers are signed. You and I are going to do a duet for my next album."

I blinked at him, damning my contract again for getting no say.

"You used to love to sing with me."

Did he see himself like I saw him? He was nothing but a marionette acting out a personality that used to be my friend. "Who are you?" I finally had to ask.

He threw me an unfriendly glare.

"I'm serious, Devon. I don't know what's happened to you. Maybe an exorcist can help or something. But whatever this thing is, it's killing you—taking you over. What will be left of you if it takes over completely?"

"I'm in control!" He shouted at me so loudly the walls echoed.

I thought back to the first night we'd met. His music had been a sort of Euro-rock-pop I'd loved in my early teens. And he'd been beautiful, sophisticated, and powerful. I'd played groupie at one of his shows to meet him and sang him a song I'd written before he could throw me to the curb for the young stalker I was.

Had it been so long ago since he'd smiled? Since that brightness had filled his eyes? How had the darkness taken him? Then the realization hit me. That first day, he hadn't been alone. In his dressing room had been a fiery redheaded woman who had been pawing through his clothes, telling him what to wear.

"It was Gina leaving you, wasn't it?"

He stiffened, but the monster remained in control. If bringing up memories about his ex-wife would help bring him back, I'd do what I had to. He couldn't keep clinging to a life he no longer had, maybe even wishing to die because he'd lost someone he'd loved.

"She still loves you, Devon. I know she does." She still handled his wardrobe, and when we used to hang out, she always came by to be sure he'd eaten. "But maybe it's time to find someone else to love."

"You volunteering?" He shuffled forward, making me back against the wall.

"I'm in love with Kerstrande."

"A vampire." He spit the words out like they had a bad taste.

"Pot, kettle." So maybe Devon didn't drink blood, but he was just as dark as KC could be—darker in fact at times, like right now.

"You know nothing."

"I know I want my friend back." I put my hands on him, reversing our roles. "So give him back to me. I want the guy who laughs and whose pretty blue eyes twinkle at my silly jokes. I want the guy who sings with everything he's ever experienced so I can compete with him. I want my mentor and friend back."

"You're just food to me." His blue eyes turned black, but I didn't try to get away. He needed help. A lot like Joel needed help. "Once I would have loved you. Now I want to eat you."

I sighed and wrapped my arms around him, letting the heat of what I was flow free through my embrace. He was so physically cold. Maybe warming him would help. He leached energy from me in large swatches, more than Cris ever had, and I knew this was something far different than an incubus, if that's what my friend called himself. Devon could suck the life out of me if he tried. Even now he glowed red with my power.

But it was my power, so I had to smile and give him exactly what he wanted. The color intensified, and he dropped to his knees, panting. This was a lot like my ability to see the dead—either I embraced it, or I ran from it. Control came from taking the reins: just a tiny release, and the oven was on.

"You burn!"

"I'm not normal. But you always knew that, ever since I told you about your dead grandmother who wanted you to know how proud she was of you. How do you think she'd feel if she could see you now? Not proud, that's for sure. I want my Devon back. Will you give him to me or make me take him from you?" I had no idea if I had the power to make whatever possessed him let him go, but I had to try.

The shadow that shrouded him peeled back slowly, and he shook with the effort. "You're just a kid."

The darkness inside him reached for me, and I shook my head. "Don't, Devon. I won't let you be the end of me. Or you." I fed the heat into him, fanned the fire to grow hotter, gave it to him to devour. The heat around him brightened to white, and I had to look away. He cried out. The light faded, leaving him looking sunburnt but no longer shrouded by the darkness. It seeped away, slinking along the floor like some dark ooze.

Devon wept. "He won't stay away forever. I've thought I've gotten away before, and he keeps coming back."

I helped my friend up. "I know. We just need to make you stronger. For now, let's sing a little, okay? I think your heart could use some lightening. I've got the perfect song for our duet." And I did, since KC had finished my graveyard song. Devon's high tenor would contrast nicely with my bass.

The rest of the day passed with me singing with the real Devon and feeling a bit more in control of my life. He'd broken down twice during the song, but we sounded really great together, switching between melody and harmony. I realized how skilled he was and I was becoming. Maybe life would begin to head in the right direction now that I was starting to fix some of the things that had been broken. When I wished Devon a good night, I hoped he'd found a little more willpower to keep moving forward too.

EVOLUTION

The glow of the microwave clock said a subway ride to the library and the cab home had taken more time than I was hoping it would. It was dark. KC hated that I was out so late. I knew the second I stepped inside that he was in a mood because the door to his study was closed. The ghosts peered at me from the bedroom, all worried, but I'd seen this show before.

I'd never entered KC's study before. In fact, I'd avoided it because he seemed to take his personal space very seriously. His introverted nature needed that separation, almost like a fortress to protect himself. But tonight I had a burning ache that had nothing to do with hormones and everything to do with the pounding of my heart.

The newspaper had been filled with PG propaganda. Attacks on vampires, pictures of people they set on fire. How any media could print that, I didn't know. Might as well post images of war zones and dead babies just for having parents of the wrong faith. It all seemed so pointless. And terrifying.

I'd agreed to an interview with a magazine reporter who wanted to talk about PG's statement about me. The world wanted me to be something other than human, so even if I said I was—and my medical records had been released to the public—they still saw what they wanted. Mr. Tokie warned me of some of the things they would ask. He even gave me a list of questions they might ask to think about for the next week, until I actually had to show up and talk face-to-face with some guy who would try to pretend he already knew me. The whole music thing was kind of frustrating. Very little of this world actually involved playing music.

I knocked lightly on the door before stepping inside. KC's computer reflected a dim glow across the room, but he hadn't bothered to turn on the overhead. The only furniture in the room was the desk and the chair he sat in. Newspapers lay scattered everywhere, with the same horrific images I tried to escape seeing each day. How much more would it take to taint that last bit of peace inside me?

He was typing something, though it didn't look like an article, since the paragraph breaks were few. His fingers flew faster than I could have ever typed, his eyes staring straight ahead like he hadn't heard me enter.

"KC?"

His shoulders stiffened, but he didn't glance back.

"Can we talk?"

"You're always talking. Didn't I tell you to be home before dark?"

"I'm home now." I stepped up beside him and eased a stack of documents onto the desk before returning to my place beside the door.

His fingers paused, but he didn't turn from the screen. I wanted to see his face. Common sense told me to stay near the door, ready to flee as the shadows converged on him. They would cover his face, that colorful array of madness, squirming like slugs over the flesh. He needed to feed, and so far had refused to bite me even though I'd offered.

"What is this?"

"The paperwork to make you a legal vampire. You just have to fill out the areas I highlighted. I already signed the donor consent form. You need to eat." The edges of fuzziness ate at my sight, but I refused to run yet. "I'll pass out if you don't eat soon. I'd rather make love to you than sleep 'cause your powers and mine don't mix well."

"That's not me, that's you."

"I'm not a vampire."

He moved so fast that suddenly he was at the door in front of me, hand over mine on the knob. I gasped. His face danced with those wicked shadows. I expected anger, but he folded his arms around me and held me against his chest, breathing heavily. His arms trembled. "I don't know if I can do it."

"KC?"

"Stop it." His voice was harsh. "Stop saying my name like that."

"Okay. Kerstrande?"

He growled. "You have no idea how hard it is not to just throw you on the ground and take you. Bleed you and leave you broken. Don't you realize that every time I touch you could be the last time you touch anyone?" He let go of me to glare at his hands. "I can't control it."

"You need to eat. I understand that. If you won't feed on me, then find someone you are willing to feed on."

He growled again.

"I wish I could make it easier on you. Is there anything I can do to help?"

"Stupid sentimentality. It doesn't go away."

That made me smile. "When it does you're no longer human. So I guess that's a good thing." I hugged him fiercely. "You're not a monster. I love you. I'm okay with you drinking my blood. I'd like not to pass out for days, though, so if we could work on that, it'd be good."

He leaned against me, finding my neck with his lips, and I stretched out for him. "You're not normal."

"Is that a bad thing?"

He sighed and finally stopped fighting. He sank his fangs into my throat while his thigh pressed against my groin. I didn't need the foreplay. Just feeling his strong mouth gulp deeply from me, knowing it was my blood that filled him, made me climax once and then race for another. The fuzziness and aggression flowed away. He licked and sucked gently at the wound until the bleeding stopped.

The hickey wasn't so bad this time. He kissed me with lips flavored with my blood and held me for some time into the night until we finally parted—me to make dinner, and him to finish writing out whatever emotional demons chased him tonight.

I was at the counter finishing dinner a little while later when KC finally said, "I'm okay with it if you want to go home."

My long blink must have told him I was confused, because he continued. "To your apartment, I mean. The one your friend lent you."

Did he want me to leave?

"I was thinking maybe we should do this the more normal way."

"This?"

"This thing between us. You know, like date and stuff. I shouldn't have just taken over everything like I did."

"I like being with you. I'm in love with you."

He stared at me. I knew that look. It was fear. This was going too fast for him, and he was freaking out. Okay, I could handle that. KC seemed to have a hard time with emotion in general and if he was feeling something for me, then of course he'd be afraid. It made me angry at Hane for playing with him to make him this way. Which reminded me of Joel. I'd have to get him out of Hane's care as soon as possible.

"Okay. Can you give me a ride later?"

Some of the tension left his shoulders. "Sure."

I let the hurt go, knowing he wasn't rejecting me. He was hiding from himself. "Will you go with me to get Joel?"

"I still don't think that's wise."

"I wouldn't have left you there either."

He sighed. "If you can prove you have control of him, you can keep him with you. If not, he'll have to stay with Hane for now. Think about this tonight, and tomorrow, if you still want to do this, I will go with you."

"Will it be safe to move him in the daytime?"

"The sunlight will make both him and Hane weaker, so if either of them attacks, we'll be better prepared."

But that meant KC would be weaker too. "Will you stay with me today? At the apartment. Cris's place, I mean. He said I could stay as long as I wanted."

KC gulped, the muscles in his long neck moving in a way that made me want to kiss him, follow those sleek lines up to his warm lips....

"I'll take you home and stop by before dawn to stay with you for the day. REA is going to take another media day. The police have been hounding them about Joel. Mr. Tokie may call you to do a last-minute interview, but there won't be any other reason for you to go to the studio."

"Okay." And just like that, I left him alone.

When he dropped me off at my apartment later, I hugged him close until he stiffened and pulled away. Sure, he wasn't good with emotions, but *I* was getting better at reading him. He played his fingers through my hair, his face was shadow-free, and he had a slight curve on his lips. He liked being with me. Maybe he wasn't in love yet, but I hoped I could bring that out of him in time.

"You'll be back later?"

"Before dawn," he promised. He glanced away and then back. "Sometimes it's just hard at night. Dealing with stuff, you know."

I nodded like I did and watched him walk away. Mikka rubbed against my leg and mewed, letting me know she was tired. "Let's get some sleep," I told her. Besides, I planned on spending a lot more intimate time with KC when he got back from wherever his brooding took him. I'd need to recharge before then.

CHAPTER 29

THE graveyard dream seemed more vivid than usual. Only the girl wasn't there. Instead it was the girl ghost from his apartment, the one who liked to talk in two word sentences. She floated right through me, which ripped me out of the graveyard and slammed me into a bedroom in a daylight suburban home. The wispy curtains rustled in the breeze, and the bed was a giant four-poster with dark wood and thick beams.

Though the place was picture-perfect enough to be in some design magazine, something about it felt wrong. The silence, maybe, or the eerie glow of the room. I didn't know. I could see a framed picture beside the bed. When I reached out to turn it my way, I was suddenly beside the nightstand staring down at it.

A wedding picture.

The man was tall, handsome, in a black tux, standing beside a beautiful woman in a white gown, both leaning in to each other for a kiss. This was the sort of thing for cake toppers and magazine photos. They could have been models, but I recognized the man in the picture.

Kerstrande. He didn't look any older than he did right now. I wondered how long he'd been a vampire. How many other lives had he survived to make it to this one? Or was he still struggling through his first? He seemed so young, so sure of himself, but something inside him connected with me.

A female hand reached around me to pick up the photo. Her long fingers and perfectly polished nails traced the image. I glanced back, and it was the girl ghost.

"He was happy once."

"You loved him."

She smiled sweetly. "Still do. Though I can't have him now. He wasn't meant to be mine anyway." Her eyes flicked in my direction, then darted away as though she were ashamed. "I lied to him. Told him I was pregnant. He turned his whole life around to be there for me. Had himself declared legally independent, though he wasn't yet eighteen. He wasn't ready to be a dad, but he was willing to try. It was the lie that Hane used to push him over the edge."

"Why did Hane change him?"

"The same reason Hane ordered Sarah to change Joel. To make you, as a band, truly immortal, legendary. He was going to do to you what he'd already done to Triple Flight. Hane is more in control of REA than he lets on."

"But KC didn't want to kill anyone, so the point was moot. He never wanted to be a vampire."

"That's where my betrayal came in handy for Hane." The room faded, and suddenly we stood in some darkened hallway of a concert venue. I didn't recognize it, which meant I probably hadn't played there yet. The girl ghost was very much alive and dressed in a short, black dress, tight and formfitting, brown hair styled up, makeup heavy, beautiful.

KC was his old rock-star self, with tight jeans and a snug T-shirt. He looked so young, and the pain in his eyes was so fresh. "This wasn't necessary," he was telling her.

"You wouldn't have married me. I was just another groupie to you."

"I've always cared about you, Anya. Ever since we were kids."

"Cared, yes, but loved, no." She turned her back on him. "I would do anything to have your baby."

"But you're not pregnant."

She spun on her heels and rushed to his side. "We could try now. Keep at it until I'm with child. I can still have your babies. Be your wife. If you keep on this path, you'll die. I've seen it. You know how I can't control the visions."

"I was trying to do the right thing, Anya. You were just trying to play me. Did you *see* this moment?"

"I love you."

He shook his head. "It's just lip service. Just like all the other groupies, record producers, and media hounds who promise pretty things while snapping pictures they'll use to insult me later." He was angry now, hurt. The set of his shoulders told me he wanted to run and hide. "I trusted you. I gave you every part of me. I made you my wife and opened myself up to you like I never have to anyone."

"But you don't love me. Your heart isn't breaking over letting me go, is it?"

"No." But the words were strained.

Hane stepped into the hallway. "We have five minutes to be on stage, Kerstrande."

KC blinked back his tears and headed toward the stage. "Goodbye, Anya."

She said nothing as he walked away.

"He was right. I'd betrayed him. I'd used his fame against him. He wasn't in love with me. He couldn't be. He was meant to love you. I saw you in his future and got so jealous...."

"You have second sight?"

"More limited than yours, but yes. I could see glimpses of the future. Read people for the most part. Except for the darkest that is. Like Hane...."

The scene changed again, this time to Hane's loft. KC sat on the floor, surrounded by unconscious women, drugs, and empty bottles of liquor. Hane sat in the corner watching. And I knew the strike would come before he even crossed the room. He'd waited for Kerstrande to be weak, to let himself wallow in despair and blind himself with pain and narcotics. They all did after a time. Artists didn't hold up well to the extreme extroverted nature required of them in the digital age. Kerstrande was no different.

I sucked in a deep breath and wished I didn't have to witness this. KC cried out from the attack. None of the girls stirred, but Hane showed no mercy.

"I can't watch this," I told Anya. "He didn't want this."

"No. But he left himself open to it. Just like Joel did. Your friend Rob is on this path as well. In time, Hane will corrupt him completely and bring him over."

"This has to stop." Wanting to play music had nothing to do with any of this pain, blood, and death.

Hane grabbed KC by the hair and dragged him down the stairs while we floated along behind him. He threw KC into the same nasty pit I'd found Joel. And Hane watched while Kerstrande's eyes lost all life and became vacant windows of death. I couldn't contain my sobs, the tears hot on my checks, though I was sure I was dreaming. It didn't matter anyway, since this was the past. This had been his first death. How many more would he suffer at Hane's hands?

I recalled the fight with Michael and how Hane had destroyed the thing Michael had become. Was KC headed for that too? Would the darkness devour him, leaving nothing but the hunger?

When the door slammed shut, KC had been good and dead. The dark brown stain seeping from him covered the floor with a stain that even years later, I hadn't been able to scrub off.

Hane peered through the window in the door as though trying to memorize the look of death. I didn't want to remember KC that way. I wanted to remember his teasing smile and the peaceful look on his face while he slept, or even the slack pleasure when we made love.

But I was standing beside a psychopath who just happened to be a vampire.

"How long did Hane leave him in there?"

"A week. The sickness usually lasts that long. The body truly dies and has to come back. Organs begin to work after days of not functioning. All that poison needs to be released from the body. That's why it's always a mess. Death is never pretty.

Death shouldn't be pretty. Especially something so violent. No wonder they had been at odds for years. Hane had murdered KC, tortured him, and made him into something that wasn't human. That was where the self-loathing came from, and the walls that seemed to be endlessly erected against the world around him.

"He wouldn't feed. He didn't want to become death. Would have rather died himself." KC hated that part of himself, the dark part that hurt others.

"The first time he took blood, he was not himself. Hane brought him a whore, someone he thought no one would miss. But that first feeding often brings back a sense of self to a vampire. Kerstrande awoke to his life as a vampire with a dead woman in his arms, her blood on his lips and in his mouth. He refused to feed again. So Hane starved him until he'd either kill someone or himself."

"You."

She nodded mournfully. "He wanted to push Kerstrande over the edge and show him the monster he'd become. I should have known. Hane's aura had always been dark, but Kerstrande trusted him. We were both fools."

The sound of footsteps echoed down that underground hall outside the room where KC was imprisoned. Hane led Anya through the darkness toward the door.

"He hasn't returned any of my calls."

"He is horribly sick. He won't let me call a doctor. I hope you can talk some sense into him." Hane opened the door and motioned her inside.

"Kerstrande?" She called out as she stepped through the doorway. Hane gave her a final shove and slammed the door shut. "Hane?"

Hane locked the door and walked away, ignoring the pounding on the door.

"I screamed for a while, more afraid of the dark than anything else. Kerstrande stalked me for a time. He'd take small bites, enough to draw blood and then back away after only a taste. I think the time had driven him mad."

"The hunger changes him. Something else takes control."

"Hane's line is from something darker. There are other vampires in the city who don't have the same shadows. But they can be beautiful."

"Like a rainbow sometimes." I shrugged. "I sort of know things are about to go bad when he gets all dark without the rainbow."

"He tore my throat out in the end. Didn't awake until the next day to realize what he'd done. But Hane opened the door to him then. Told him that it was time to live or die. To live and learn to hunt, or to die in the filth of the pit. I was one of the first, but not the last."

"He tried to reprogram KC to be a monster. But he's stronger now. He doesn't have to kill, and doesn't kill…."

"It happens. He hates to feed, so he puts it off until the darkness overtakes him. If you can keep him fed, he will stop killing. I think for the first time he has a reason to live, and to learn how to control the need."

But KC kept pushing me away. He'd fed for the first time in a while tonight because I'd pushed him and because he'd waited almost too long. He couldn't keep doing that. If he let the hunger take over, he'd lose control. He admitted that himself. Hane had trained him that the hunger was awful, and starving himself until he killed was the best way. I just had to teach him otherwise.

And KC wasn't the only one in Hane's hands. He wasn't the only one Hane abused. How many others? When would it end? I took a deep breath and turned to Anya. "It has to end. I have to go get Joel."

"He won't let Joel go. He won't let Kerstrande go."

He would. I would make him. "He's a monster."

"Yes."

"I have to go now. I'm sorry, Anya."

She smiled. "I'm sorry too. I wish Kerstrande could have loved me the way he loves you."

My heart skipped a beat hearing those words, but I needed them to come from KC, not his dead wife's ghost. "He doesn't love me yet. But someday soon, I hope he will." One problem at a time.

CHAPTER 30

THE memory of the dream kept me on edge while a cab drove me to Hane's place. I knew I should have waited until the daytime. But I couldn't let KC face him again. Each time they saw each other, it was like a stab into his very soul. The time for Hane to cause KC pain had to end.

I paid the cab driver and told him not to wait. Instead I called Cris, who didn't answer, but I left a message anyway. If something happened to me tonight, at least one person would know. On the counter in the apartment, I'd left a long note for KC, just in case. Even if he never believed I really loved him, I would tell him with my dying breath. Maybe someday it would sink into that thick skull of his.

The place was dark as usual, but the door was unlocked. Was Hane expecting me? I didn't bother to go up the stairs. Instead I headed down, using the heat I could project to burn through the gate and leave it open so we would have a means of escape. I had to get Joel out first; then I could confront Hane.

The stench hadn't lightened at all. I wondered if Hane saw himself as some sort of undead mobster and just executed people regularly down here when they got in the way. Did vampires have

213

different politics? I didn't think KC would answer if I asked, or even if he knew. Maybe Cris knew something.

I heard a scratching noise before I even got close to the steel door that locked Joel inside. "Joel?"

The scratching stopped.

"Are you okay in there? I've come back to take you home with me." I dropped the backpack filled with clothes for him by the wall, praying nothing crawled into it while I was saving Joel from himself. I really hoped he hadn't trashed the room again. "Joel?"

The silence was so loud I wanted to scream. Damn. I yanked on the lock, finally getting it to ease open. Joel spilled out like he'd been leaning on the door. His hands were bloody, nails torn to shreds. The back of the door was covered in red streaks. I sighed and pulled my friend to his feet.

"We have to go now."

"Hungry," he whispered.

I stopped moving and had to look at him again. Was there someone home this time, or was that just the shadows talking?

"A sip. That's all." I held my wrist up to his lips.

"Sip," he breathed against my skin just before his fangs sunk in.

It hurt more the second time than it had the first. But I counted to thirty, thinking about how much I wanted my friend Joel back, and then tugged my arm away. He let me go, lapping at the last few drops like a cat with milk.

"Sip," he said again.

"Yeah, that was a sip. We have to go home now."

"Not a good idea," Hane said as lights lit up the hallway. "I've already told you he's not right." He moved toward us like he couldn't care what we did.

"Then why didn't you put him down? Why keep him here like some sort of pet? Abuse him like you did Kerstrande? What's the point?"

EVOLUTION

"Because I enjoy breaking the strong. Sadly, your friend Joel was weak. I'd rather break you." Hane stood before us looking like whatever had been eating Devon had devoured him instead. Blackness, death, shadows, pain, hunger, and rage, they were not a pretty combination. "He belongs to me." He pointed to Joel. "Just as Kerstrande does."

"They are people."

"They are animals."

I looked at Joel, and all I saw was the friend I'd lost. Even though he'd stained KC's sweater in blood and still looked pale enough to not pass for anything other than dead, he was still Joel. Maybe not quite human anymore, but he was still a person.

Joel blinked at me like he wasn't really seeing me, but I helped him lean against the wall. If this was going to be a blowout between Hane and me, I hoped to save Joel first. He could tell what had happened. Make sure the world knew what Hane had done. Keep him from doing it to others.

"Let us go, Hane. Let KC go. They mean nothing to you. They mean everything to me."

"They are already dead. Why don't you join them?"

"Because I'm not willing to be your plaything."

"Death does not wait." He smiled and then a half second later had me shoved into the wall, fangs in my neck. I struggled to breathe.

I pounded on his back, trying to loosen his grip, but he gulped at my throat, sucking down my blood like his very life depended on it. He gripped my arm hard. The bone snapped with a loud crack, and I couldn't keep from crying out painfully. "Stop!"

Something large and heavy smashed into Hane from the side, and I sunk to the ground, hands over my neck, praying he hadn't hit something vital as blood streamed over my fingers. How soon would it take me to bleed out?

The pain in my arm pulsed in throbs. I curled around it like I could stop if from hurting by just willing it to. The heat of my blood

215

stung as it dripped through my fingers. Each drop sizzled when it hit the ground. It hadn't been that hot when Joel had bitten me. Was I dying again? Somehow I didn't think changing into a flaming bird was going to help us much.

Joel worried away at Hane's arm like he was some sort of dog. Hane smashed him away only to have the man rebound and hit him harder with all teeth and claws. The two rolled around for a bit, hitting each other and growling. Darkness began to box in my sight. Was this to be the end, then?

I thought about the heat that filled me and how I could change. The last time I had died to complete the change. What would happen if I died again?

Joel hit the wall just a few feet from me and stayed still. I couldn't find the strength to move toward him to see if he was alive. But anger filled me with a burning heat. I wanted to rip Hane apart for hurting Joel, KC, and probably killing me.

Him stalking toward me, with deliberately slow movements, was the last thing I saw before fire exploded around me. I willed it into him, wanting to give him the pain and the heat. The flames ate up my vision, and all I felt for a few seconds was peace.

Then the screaming began.

At first I thought it was me, but no, someone else was on fire. The world around me darkened for just a minute. No dreams this time. Just one second there was fire, the next I was inhaling smoke and choking. Something was holding me, and the grip hurt. I cried out, but the sound wasn't human.

"It's okay, Gene. Just calm your pet vampire down, and we'll all leave."

The semipanicked words made me rub my eyes to clear my vision. Only instead of hands, I had feathers again. Damn.

Cris stood only a few feet away. He held a blanket in his arms and had both hands out in front of him like he was trying to prove he was harmless. The hands that held me too tightly were Joel's.

"Concentrate on being human, Genesis. You can turn back. I think you can control him. He's protecting you, which is great, but we should get out of here since the police are coming, and the building is on fire."

I tried to remember what it was like to have limbs instead of wings. The weight of my body returned, and it hurt this time, like a really bad sunburn. Joel had a death grip on my arm. I turned and looked him in the eye, and for the first time, I recognized the light that resided there. My friend was in there. Thank God!

I threw my arms around him.

"Wow, naked man," Joel muttered, voice hoarse.

Cris offered me the blanket. It was better than nothing. The stench hit me as I was tying the sheet in place. Burned flesh and hair, like meat, only something much worse.

"Don't look, Gene. It's not worth the nightmares," Cris warned me.

"The fire came from the inside," Joel said. "He burned slower than you. You went up so fast I thought you were gone."

My blood.

I had to look. The blackened shell couldn't be anything other than what was left of Hane. He still smoked and smoldered, a crispy skeleton. The fire had jumped to him probably because I'd willed it to. My blood set him on fire because I wanted him to hurt. I'd done that.

My stomach clenched, and I dry heaved while Cris held me up. The sounds of sirens echoed throughout the building, and then, distantly, the sound of a fire truck.

"We need to go." Cris dragged me toward the door.

"This way." Joel pointed in another direction.

We followed him. Well, Cris followed, tugging me the whole way. I couldn't do anything other than cry. I'd killed Hane. What was wrong with me? What did I really think would happen when I came here determined to get Joel out?

The truth was that I had expected to die.

And I had, hadn't I? But I wasn't normal. Just like KC always said.

CHAPTER 31

I KNEW before we even got out of the car that KC was already upstairs. His car was in the underground garage. The drive had been long enough for me to nap. Joel had startled me awake twice with the constant jittery movements he'd done when he was human. At least he was acting more like himself. He sat in back with me, curled up against my side, even though we had the whole seat to ourselves.

When we parked, Cris helped me to the elevator, and up we went, Joel following like a trained dog. The double metal doors opened to my floor, and I saw Kerstrande leaning against the wall outside my borrowed apartment.

"KC." I tried to reach for him but tripped over the blanket I had tied on and would have landed on my face if Joel and Cris hadn't held me up.

Kerstrande was suddenly beside me. "What the hell happened?"

His hands cupped my face, and I couldn't stop from saying, "Ow."

"Why is his skin burnt?" KC looked at the two men with me.

"He burst into flames," Joel said.

"Hane killed him. Fed on him. I think when Gene went up in flames, the blood that Hane ingested ignited too. By the time I got down the stairs, they were both already on fire." Cris let go of my arm, and I dropped into KC's embrace.

KC's face turned to a mass of rainbow color slugs, and I knew he was mad. "Sorry I didn't wait for you. I couldn't let him hurt you anymore. Not after the way he used Anya to destroy you. I'm not Anya, KC. I'm not Hane or Michael. I'm not here to hurt you, and I will take the pain from you when I can."

"You stupid fool!"

"Hey now," Cris tried to interrupt.

"Butt out!"

"KC—" I tried to speak, but his lips covered mine. And we were suddenly kissing in the hallway, with my ex-lover Cris and my friend and bandmate, Joel, staring down at us. This was so far beyond what I knew from KC that I just let him go on. But it felt like he wanted to devour me.

When the kiss finally ended, he was crying.

"I'm okay," I whispered to him, feeling his arms wrap around me and hold me almost painfully tight. "I'm so sorry." Since it was nearly four in the morning, the halls were still empty, but none of us seemed willing to move.

"We should take this inside," Cris said quietly. "People will be up soon." He moved toward the door, even fishing out a key to open it before motioning us inside.

KC scooped me up into his arms and carried me toward the apartment. "You have to invite me in. The monster movies got that right. You have to invite death in."

"You're not death, KC. I love you. I trust you, and I invite you into my home." I glanced at Joel. "I invite you in, Joel."

We crossed the threshold together. He sat down on the couch, me still in his arms. Cris took the chair, and Joel began to pace the room. The shadows on KC's face faded away, and finally he sat back, let my head rest on his chest, and said, "Tell me again, slowly, exactly what happened."

EVOLUTION

Everyone took turns. I fell asleep somewhere in the middle of Cris's version. When next I awoke it was in bed, with KC wrapped around me. The window was covered, and though I didn't see any spirits, I knew they lingered because there was an unnatural chill to the air.

"You might as well show yourselves," I muttered to the room, hoping I didn't wake KC. The ghosts filled the room again. Anya hovered near the bed, looking normal instead of grisly dead. "Anya."

"It's time for me to go, Genesis. Kerstrande is letting me go."

I breathed a sigh of relief. Maybe he would let go of all the guilt now. But while Anya looked good and normal, shining like a star, the rest still looked like death warmed over. I hope I didn't have to kill another vampire for every one of the spirits that haunted KC. I was pretty sure my karma would get tipped the wrong way.

Anya faded, and the rest seemed to move on for the night. I watched him sleep for a few minutes.

"That's kind of creepy."

I jumped a half foot in the air, then playfully smacked KC for scaring me. "That was awful."

"You're the one staring at me."

"You're so beautiful when you sleep."

He snorted.

"You are." I set my head on the pillow beside him and let myself just rest with his breath and mine mingling. At least vampires could still breathe, and I knew his heart beat because I could feel it against my palm. "I love you, KC."

"So you keep telling me."

"I died for you."

"No one asked you to." Mr. Grumpy-Pants was back.

I couldn't help but laugh. And the laughter turned to hysterics because I laughed so hard I could hardly breathe.

"Quiet down. Your friends are sleeping in the spare room and on the couch."

I swallowed back the rest of my laughter but couldn't help but grin at him.

"You're such a brat."

"But you love me anyway," I taunted him.

"Yeah, I do."

The words took a minute to sink in, but then at that moment, nothing else mattered as much as the man in my arms.

Kerstrande

THE shovel hit the casket. I scrapped away the dirt from the fancy cover. Aaron had arranged a beautiful box, a huge ceremony, even a tribute like Michael's. Only Evolution wasn't going to play at this one. In fact, almost no one would be grieving Hane Lewis. The days of Triple Flight were over forever, and I was here to ensure it stayed that way.

Four days would have been enough time for him to awaken. Maybe even heal a bit and try to get out. I should have left him. A few centuries in the box might mellow him out a bit. Or make him crazier. And Hane had always been a sick fuck anyway. When the cops showed up after the fire was put out, they found bodies. Lots of bodies, stacked in several rooms.

Newspapers had labeled him the "Killer Rock Star," and PG was using this to fan their rage against anything not pure, white, and human. Most of the victims had multiple bites. Many had been failed attempts to bring over a new vampire. The cages of feral vampires had slaughtered a half dozen cops. The ACLU was going crazy trying to defend the vampires from a death sentence. They would start with Joel, who had turned himself in at Gene's request. He was awaiting a trial and was expected to be allowed to live. I had a feeling it would hurt Genesis pretty bad if his keyboardist died.

Damon Phillis, the American King of vampires, had called with questions about Hane's death. Mostly because he knew Hane wasn't dead yet, and I wasn't strong enough to hold a city this size. The little time I'd been undead didn't give me that kind of strength, but Genesis did. Regular infusions of his blood helped control the bloodlust. Killing Hane for real would give me control of the rest of the vampires in the city, and enough power to actually stay there. Phillis had already threatened to send someone else to the city to take over. As if I really needed the threat.

The late morning hours ticked past the witching hour. Not a single soul ventured into this cemetery. It was for the damned. No crosses or priests or angels. Just the dead and unwanted. I'd have to hurry if I wanted to be back by the time Gene got up for work.

The lock broke easily enough, and I snapped it open to stare at the shriveled form within. It didn't move. Even the undead had a pulse; slower than the living, but if I waited long enough I would hear it. I leaned in to listen for the sound.

A crisp black hand snaked around my throat, cutting off my air. I rewarded him with a solid face-pounding. He let go, whimpering, skull cracked in several places. "Hello, Hane. You look like shit."

"Fuck you."

"You've been trying for years, and I'm still not interested." I grabbed him by the neck and began to squeeze. "Game over, you son of a bitch. The city is mine now."

"You can't handle the darkness, Kerstrande. It will take over, and you will kill your beloved pop star yourself."

"In case you haven't noticed, Gene is pretty good at taking care of himself. Since he flambéed you and all." I scraped at the flaking skin on his chest, which had him shrieking.

He sucked in deep breaths. "Michael should never have asked me to change you."

"Don't blame this on Michael." We'd been childhood friends, best friends. Probably much like Gene and Rob had been at one time. But just like them, we'd gone our separate ways, grown as different individuals who didn't share the same goals. Michael had become the killer Hane always wanted him to be, but I never had.

"He wanted you with him always. You were like his big brother, his mentor, but you were going to throw it all away. Die so others wouldn't have to. But we all die in the end."

"We don't need to kill, Hane. That's what you never got. It wasn't about the death. It was all about the blood." Even now it was about the blood. Mine. Genesis's. And Hane's. Yeah, I'd need his blood to take over the city.

"You've wanted to die for years. Have been killing yourself slowly for years."

"I'm okay with dying. It's living that's a bitch."

To Be Continued....

SAM KADENCE has always dreamed about being someone else, somewhere else. With very little musical talent, Sam decided the only way to make those dreams come true was to try everything from cosplay at the local anime conventions to writing novels about pretending to run away to become a musician.

Sam has a Bachelor's degree in Creative Writing, sells textbooks for a living, enjoys taking photographs of Asian Ball Joint Dolls to tell more stories, and has eclectic taste in music from J-pop to rock and country. All of which finds its way into the books eventually.

Facebook: https://www.facebook.com/SamKadence

The Unlikely Hero
The Verses of Vrelenden: Book One
Beau Schemery

Harmony Ink

CPSIA information can be obtained at www.ICGtesting.com
Printed in the USA
LVOW01s1535130114

369231LV00023B/1499/P